VIOLENT THINGS

VIOLENT THINGS

Copyright © 2015 Callie Hart All rights reserved.

No part of this publication may be reproduced, distributed, or transmitted in any form or by any means, including photocopying, recording, or other electronic or mechanical methods, without the prior written permission of the author, except in the case of brief quotations embodied in critical reviews and certain other noncommercial uses permitted by copyright law.

For permission requests, write to the author, addressed "Attention: Permissions Coordinator," at callie.law.author@gmail.com

This is a work of fiction. Any resemblance to peoples either living or deceased is purely coincidental. Names, places and characters are figments of the author's imagination, or, if real, used fictitiously. The author recognises the trademarks and copyrights of all registered products and works mentioned within this work.

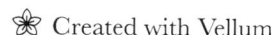

❃ Created with Vellum

1

SLOANE

You can't tell someone not to die just because it's Christmas Eve. I should know. I've tried twice already and it hasn't worked either time. St. Peter's has been non-stop since I started my shift thirty-six hours ago, and it doesn't look like things are going to quiet down any time soon.

Zeth is going to kill me. I was supposed to be home nearly twelve hours ago, but the gunshot wound, alcohol poisoning and bar fight victims have kept on rolling in. Now, Mikey the intern and I are waiting on the tarmac outside the hospital for the second road traffic accident of the night and my body is humming. It's close to midnight. I should be exhausted, but the adrenalin that's helped me act fast and think quick on the trauma floor has me wired.

"You think it'll stop snowing soon?" Mikey asks. "I'm supposed to drive out to Snoqualmie Pass after this. The roads are gonna be closed at this rate."

"Hate to break it to you, buddy, but the roads are already closed." I slap Mikey on the back, giving him my best consolatory look. I heard them read out the list of closures on the radio at the nurses' station earlier in the night, waiting with bated breath to see if the access road up to my own house was still open. Thankfully it is. Unlucky for Mikey, though. He's shit out of luck.

"Ahhh fuck, man. My whole family are up there already. I'm gonna be eating baked beans on toast for Christmas dinner tomorrow. *Alone.*"

"Better get used to it. Being a doctor generally means you don't get Christmas. Or Easter. Or Thanksgiving. Or your birthday. Basically we don't get anything."

"Perfect." Mikey sulks while we wait, the big fat flakes of snow falling silently all around us. It's like we're trapped inside a snow globe; everything is so still. That is until I see the flashing lights of the ambulance rig tearing up the road toward us.

"Here we go. Incoming." I glance over my shoulder just as Oliver Massey runs out of the building behind me, huge clouds of fog billowing on his breath. He's pulling on a set of rubber gloves, squinting up the road, searching for the ambo.

"Sorry, the kid I was closing up crashed. Took a while to stabilize. What we got?"

"Two patients," Mikey says. "Woman, early thirties, with potential spinal injury and severe blood loss. Also, one of the firefighters who responded to the call. He was sliding in through the passenger window of the car the other patient was trapped inside of. The streetlight she hit fell down on top of the vehicle. He has a head injury, broken leg and possible internal bleed.

"Ah. Right, well I guess that explains the fire truck then," Oliver says. Sure enough, there's a fire truck bringing in the ambulance, full lights and sirens blaring out into the night. The two emergency service vehicles tear into the parking lot, the fire truck pulling up outside the unloading bay, while the ambo brakes right at the door.

Oliver and Mikey rush forward with a gurney while I hurry to talk to the female EMT who's jumping down from the rig. "There should be another ambulance. Where's our second patient?"

"On their way. The roads are crazy. We're lucky *we* made it here in one piece." "Who have you got?"

"Alex Massey, lieutenant over at firehouse sixty-three. He was awake when we loaded him up, but he lost consciousness shortly after. He's systolic. Blood pressure's through the floor. We pushed dopamine en route."

"Alright, we'd better move quickly then. We need to find out what's going on inside."

Oliver and Mikey are already rushing the gurney with the injured firefighter into St. Peter's. Oliver's face is ashen, white as a sheet. "I'm gonna need you to scrub in on this one, Sloane," he tells me.

"I can't, I'm point on trauma tonight. I need to oversee the emergency—"

"Sloane, you're fucking scrubbing in. I need you. I need *you*."

"Olly—"

"It's my brother, Sloane. *It's my fucking brother.*"

I get Dr. Tarney to take over trauma for me and I do scrub in. There's no way Oliver should be operating on his own brother—it goes against every rule the hospital has—but there's no stopping him. By the time the chief knows Alex

Massey is in need of medical attention, he's already receiving it.

We're fighting to find the source of Alex's extensive internal bleeding when the chief storms into the OR, a surgical mask covering her face. "Dr. Massey? Dr. Massey, you need to step away from that patient right now," she says calmly.

Oliver's working like a man possessed, though. There's no way he's going to do that. "I'm afraid things are a little critical in here right now, Chief. You'll have to excuse me if I decline."

"Dr. Massey, I'm already scrubbed. I can take over from you. You need to leave. *Now.*"

Oliver glances up at me, asking me a silent question—do I have his back? I nod. Some doctors would fall apart in situations like this, but not Olly. He's galvanized, working methodically. He's not showing any signs of being emotionally compromised. If he were, I'd be the first person to agree with the chief. As it stands, I say, "He's got this, Chief. Dr. Massey's currently stemming an aortic bleed. If he lets go—"

"I can catch it. Oliver. I'm serious. This is not how we work."

Oliver frowns, still entirely focused on his work. "Are you the best cardiothoracic surgeon in this hospital?" His voice is totally steady.

The chief doesn't say anything.

"Because the last time I checked, you were the best *pediatric* surgeon in this hospital and I'd just been promoted to the head of my department. Which just so happens to be cardiothoracics."

"*Oliver.*"

"I have this under control, Chief. Now if you'll excuse me, I have to concentrate on not letting my brother's heart tear itself apart."

The chief gives me a stern look—I'm still not forgiven for the crazy shit I was caught up in a couple of months ago, and aligning myself with a disobedient Oliver won't have helped matters. "Fine," she snaps. "But I'll be watching every single move you make." The chief huffs out an exasperated breath and backs out of the room, hitting the exit button with her elbow in order to keep the room sterile.

Oliver looks up at me once she's gone. "Thank you."

"Just save him, okay. I'm gonna be working extra shifts in the VD clinic to make up for this." I must be out of my mind. Don't rock the boat: that's what I tell myself every time I step foot through the hospital doors, and what is it I end up doing? Rocking the goddamn boat. Nearly capsizing the goddamn boat.

"Is she up there?" Oliver asks, his eyes darting upward to the observation gallery.

I look up in time to see the chief fling open the door to the glass box above us. The surgical mask is gone, which allows me to see her whole facial expression— how truly furious she is. She glowers at me as she sits down next to…as she sits down next to *Zeth*.

"*Fuck*." I whisper it under my breath. What the hell is he *doing* here?

"Ahhh shit. Sloane, something's not right. I thought I'd stemmed the flow, but there's more blood now. It's not coming from the heart. We need to find it."

Zeth is forgotten. The observation gallery may as well not exist as I fix every last ounce of concentration on the problem at hand. Oliver and I keep our heads down as we both work in unison, part of a well-oiled machine, trying to find the source of Alex's bleeding.

It turns out to be a perforation in his lower intestine. Not a usual cause for so much blood, especially seeping into the chest cavity, but the damage is severe.

We resect a good portion of Alex's lower bowel, scrambling to save every millimeter we can. Alex is a firefighter. I don't know him, but I can guarantee he won't want a colostomy bag.

Hours slip by. We manage to preserve enough bowel to avoid having to instal a stoma right away, but only time will tell on that front. If Alex develops an infection and the tissue doesn't heal, we may have to revisit that idea.

Oliver is swaying on his feet by the time we close his brother. I'm fine, clear--headed and alert, until we stitch Alex up and let the nurses take over. Exhaustion hits me like a brick wall to the face as soon as my responsibility to my patient is over, though. I feel drunk as Oliver and I strip off our surgical gloves, masks and gowns and throw them in the HAZMAT bins.

Outside the OR, Oliver loses it. His composure abandons him as he slides down the wall and begins to cry. "Oh my god. Olly, he's gonna be fine. You did a good job. Hey, don't worry." I crouch down and wrap my arms around him, holding him to me as his body shakes. I know this meltdown isn't about fear for Alex's safety. The guy should be okay, providing nothing awful happens. This is just shock. The pressure of having to keep himself together for so many hours has taken its toll.

"Thank you. Thank you. I wouldn't have trusted anybody else," Oliver says, drawing in a deep breath. "Fuck, this is stupid." He dashes away his tears with the backs of his hands, and then heaves himself to his feet. His face reddens a little when he looks back over my shoulder. "I think I've monopolized enough of your time, Romera. Looks like you're needed elsewhere."

Zeth is leaning against the wall down the corridor, hands in his pockets, watching us. He looks down at his feet when he sees he's been spotted.

"Yeah, I swore I'd be home for Christmas day," I say.

"Then you should go." Oliver gives me a gentle shove in the back.

I really should, too. Zeth has never once broken a promise he's made to me. I aim on honoring my promises right back. "If anything happens, you know you can just call me right away," I tell Oliver.

"I do."

"Okay. I'll see you in a couple of days, Ol." I head off down the corridor, but he calls out to me, stopping me before I reach Zeth.

"Hey, Romera?"

"Yeah?"

He gives me a halfhearted, weak smile. "Merry Christmas, right?"

"Yeah. Merry Christmas, Ol."

2

ZETH

She looks like she's ready to pass the fuck out. I think I'm gonna have to catch her when she collapses against me, face pressed into my chest, but I don't. She's just tired and leaning on me. I fold my arms around her and hold her up anyway, because that's what I'm here for. Always. Being there for her to lean on will be my primary job from now and until the day I die, and boy do I have a serious case of job satisfaction.

"You okay?" I breathe into her hair.

She nods, grunting something inaudible into my leather jacket. I kiss her on the top of her head, smoothing down the strands that have escaped her ponytail.

"I'm taking you home now, angry girl. You got anything to say about that?"

She looks up at me, eyes already drooping, and gives me a lazy smile. "I say thank god for that."

She falls asleep in the car, forehead pressed up against the cold glass of the passenger window, and I can't fucking help myself. At every available opportunity, I find myself looking at her out of the corner of my eye. I need to make sure this miraculous woman is real.

I saw it the first time at Julio's compound when Carnie brought Alexis in and laid her out on the table. Sloane was a force of nature, unstoppable and single-minded as she worked over her sister's broken body.

She'd saved Alexis's life when she would have died otherwise, no two ways about it. Watching her then had taken my breath away. The same thing happened tonight, watching her work over the guy on the table in that operating room. She didn't hesitate. She didn't stop and she did not once give up. Not even when the chief of medicine, sitting next to me, had started swearing like a marine when the guy had coded not once but twice.

My angry girl is a fucking hero.

The ugly ass Hummer Rebel left behind with us in Seattle struggles to make it up the narrow, winding road to our house as we leave the city. Snow coats everything—the road, the trees, the mountains in the distance. The whole world is white under the headlights of the car as I drive us back to the warmth of home.

She's still sleeping when I pull up outside. I don't have the heart to wake her, so I take off my jacket and put it over her as I lift her out of the car and carry her carefully inside.

The fire's gone out, but Ernie's still coiled up in a ball in front of the embers. He lifts his head when we come inside, but he doesn't bark. Terrible fucking guard dog he'd make. I think we've accepted the fact that Ernie's more likely to studiously ignore an intruder than attack them.

I carry Sloane past the long forgotten arrangements I'd made to surprise her when she came home, straight up the stairs and into the bedroom. I strip her of her clothes as carefully as I can, fingertips grazing the rise and swell of her breasts as I do —sue me, I'm not a fucking saint—and then I tuck her up under the sheets, warring with myself. I want to wake her up and fuck her. I also want her to be fully compos mentis the next time I screw her, so I manage to keep my dick in my pants. Fucking St. Peter's Hospital. The place is determined to ruin my sex life.

Instead of accosting her in her sleep, I leave Sloane to her dreams and head back downstairs. The table is exactly how I left it, except now the food is stone cold and the candles have all guttered out. Did I cook for her? Hell fucking no. But you'd better believe I tried, and when that failed, ordered in her favorite Thai food. The Pad Thai looks like a congealed mess on the plate now. I collect everything up and toss it into the trash, kind of glad she didn't make it back in time.

I'd been impulsive. I was going to do something rash, and now I'm a little fucking relieved things didn't work out the way I was planning. After seeing Sloane at the hospital tonight, the last thing she needs is me acting like a lovesick teenager, making rash calls and disrupting her shit. She needs to focus. She needs to concentrate on being the best she can be at her job. I won't stand in the way of that. Not again.

I hang up my leather jacket, removing the gift I'd planned on giving her tonight from the pocket. I close my fist around it, shaking my head, wondering what the hell I was thinking. The gift goes into the back of a drawer behind a stack of papers, and I put it out of my mind.

I tell myself that I do.

But when I go to sleep, hand lying heavy on Sloane's hip, I have a dream. It's not a dream about fighting in the dark, and it's not a dream about my mother crying in the front seat of a car. It's a dream of something much sweeter.

SLOANE

There used to be a time when my boyfriend wouldn't sleep in the same bed as me. There are still nights when he's particularly restless and I'll wake to find him gone, but this morning I know he's still with me. I know because the heavy weight of his arm is over me and I feel like I'm being pinned to the mattress.

I don't even attempt to move. It's not as though I feel trapped. Rather, I feel safe, so why would I want to escape? I close my eyes and allow myself to drift, listening to the muffled sounds of snow sliding off the roof mixed in with Zeth's even, steady breathing.

This is what heaven feels like. By the time dawn breaks properly, I can sense that he's waking up. He doesn't shift or tighten his grip around me. The rhythm of his breathing remains the same. I'm just suddenly aware that he is *there*, his consciousness present alongside mine, whereas before it wasn't.

After a long time, he rolls his head across his pillow so he can lay a kiss on my shoulder. "Merry Christmas, Dr. Romera," he tells me, his voice husky from sleep.

"Merry Christmas to you, too." I wriggle backward, butt first, nestling into the curve of his body, and he lets out a sleep filled groan.

"You keep doing that and you'll be having problems walking for the rest of the holidays."

"I have a few days off." I bite my lip, trying to hide the smile from my voice. "Walking's overrated anyway."

"Is that so?" He leans down and kisses me on my shoulder again, but this time he teases his teeth across my skin, biting me lightly. His arm snakes around my waist, taking hold of me. "Michael's coming over this morning. I'm gonna call and tell him not to bother."

"Don't you dare. It's Christmas day and he stayed back in Seattle to help you with the gym. We're his family here. He's spending Christmas day with us."

Zeth grumbles inarticulate things into my neck. I think some of it might have something to do with Rebel being an asshole and not looking after his family. As Zeth's hot breath skims over my skin, his hands are skimming other parts of my body. Quick, sure fingers travel down my stomach, over my hip, where he lightly teases them over my thigh and up in between my legs.

"Spread them for me," he growls, deep and low into my ear. I have no problem hearing him this time. I open my legs at his first request, not needing to be told more than once. Zeth makes a pleased sound of approval at the back of his throat. His hands continue on their journey around my body, this time taking a detour in between my thighs, upward, so his fingertips graze against the fine material of my panties. "Are you ready for your Christmas present, Sloane?"

As if he needs to ask. My breathing's already quickened, my pulse rate speeding away from me. I nod quickly, wrapping my hand around his forearm, willing him to just do it—to touch the hypersensitive point between my legs, where it feels like every single nerve ending in my body originates. "Depends what you've got for me," I say. "And if you're planning on making me beg for it."

Zeth is fully awake now. I can tell by the way his muscles have tensed, his body hardening against mine. All of it. I can feel the rigid pressure of his hard-on pressing up against my ass. "You'll never have to beg me for what I'm about to give you, angry girl. Misbehave badly enough and you can have it whenever you want it. Wait here."

He springs out of bed, throwing the covers aside so that a blast of cold air hits my back. It's chilly outside of our little cocoon of blankets, and I immediate miss his hot skin on me. He pads barefoot across the room, the muscles in his back shifting beautifully as he walks. His naked ass—he refuses to sleep in clothes, even though it's the dead of winter—is the very definition of perfection. He laughs a wicked laugh as he pulls…*as he pulls out his black duffel bag from the bottom of the wardrobe*. My heart starts knocking against my ribcage like it's trying to get out.

"What are you doing?" I ask warily.

When he turns around, Zeth is working his fist up and down his hard-on, grinning darkly. "What does it look like I'm doing?"

I don't bother answering him. I push myself up

in the bed, half considering leaping out of bed and making a break for it. I get like this—a thrill of adrenalin zips through my body every time I see that damn bag sitting there in the bottom of our wardrobe. I'm always either stopping myself from opening it up or stopping myself from running away.

"Have you been a good girl this year, Sloane?" Zeth rumbles, stalking his way toward the bed. Toward *me*. "Or have you been…*bad*?"

I cover my mouth with my fingers, holding my breath. "What's the right answer here? I get the feeling there isn't one."

A moderately sinister smile spreads across my boyfriend's face. He's reached the bed now. He's lowering the bag down onto the foot of it, moving with calculated caution as he takes hold of the handle and slowly begins to unzip…

"It doesn't really matter," he says. "You're getting the same treatment either way. Close your eyes."

We play this game of chicken, where I pretend I'm braver than he thinks I am, and I do everything he asks me to first time. Today it's much harder to comply, though. I'm a little perturbed by whatever he might be pulling out of that duffel this morning.

"*Sloane?*" Zeth tips his head to one side, lifting

an eyebrow. I close my eyes, my pulse throbbing in every part of my body as the bed dips and he climbs up onto it. "Open your mouth, angry girl," he whispers.

I do it. I can taste the saltiness of him as he teases the very tip of his cock over my lips. Over the tip of my tongue. This…this is something I can handle quite happily. I duck my head forward, ready to take all of him into my mouth, but Zeth grabs a handful of my hair and jerks me back.

"*Ah ah ah.* You haven't earned that yet."

"Fucking—" I bite back the urge to call him something bad.

Zeth stoops down over me, pulling at my lower lip with his teeth. "Such a dirty mouth."

There are a million comments I could come back with here, but I know him. He's in a playful mood and I don't want to rile him. I gasp, flinching against the delicious pain of his teeth pulling at my flesh, his hand pulling at my hair.

He draws back a second later, and then I feel the cold, hard sting of steel against the skin of my wrists.

Handcuffs. Zeth cuffs my hands over my head, making appreciative noises as the covers fall away from my body to reveal my naked breasts. The cold doesn't seem to matter anymore. All that matters is what Zeth pulls out of that bag next.

He doesn't make me wait long. The rest of the covers are ripped from the bed, and then it's just me cuffed to the headboard, vulnerable and on show, while he positions himself over me. "You want this, angry girl?" he whispers, his breath hot and fast against my cheek.

I nod, my head swimming with the need to open my eyes. That's part of the game, though. If I open them, I've disobeyed him. If I resist and keep them closed, I've done as I'm told.

These days, half the game is waiting to find out whether I'm going to be receiving pain or pleasure. I've given up pretending that I prefer the later. I'm always torn between the two, wanting the delirium of the pleasure washing over me, but also the furious sting of the pain lighting my body up and making me come alive. It's almost as though I can't have one without the other these days.

I nearly jump out of my skin when Zeth presses something cool and hard against the inside of my leg. "I need you on your front," he tells me. "Be a good girl and get up onto your knees. *Now.*"

I spin over, my wrists twinging a little as the cuffs dig into my skin.

"Good. Now spread those legs for me. And bend over."

Heat flushes up through me, half embarrassment, half anticipation. I have absolutely no reason to be embarrassed anymore. Zeth's explored every single part of my body from every single angle possible, but exposing myself to him like this is always a little confronting. He hums as he places his hands on my ass and lowers himself, ducking down so he can run his tongue over the very center of me, licking my pussy.

"So. Fucking. Sweet," he growls.

He loves going down on me, has done since our very first encounter. My body is shaking with the tense pleasure of his tongue working over me by the time he decides I've had enough. He straightens himself up and leans into me, resting his cock against my ass cheeks.

"Still got those eyes closed, angry girl?" he rumbles into my ear.

"Yes," I pant.

"Good girl. Such a good girl." He's moving, then, sliding something chilled and solid up the inside of my leg again. It starts to vibrate as he pushes it against the entrance of my pussy. "Get ready," he tells me. "This is gonna feel very…*full*."

He slides whatever he has in his hand—a vibrator, must be—further, further, further inside me until the hilt of it is pressing up against my clit. The intensity of the vibrations increases, sending a shockwave of pleasure rippling over my skin. "Oh...my...*god*."

"We're not finished yet," Zeth says. I understand immediately after what he has planned. He thrusts his hips against my ass, the tip of his cock sliding down between my ass cheeks, and I draw in a sharp, nervous breath. I haven't done this before. Not with something already inside me.

"Trust me?" Zeth asks, pushing a little harder.

I try to slow the thunder of my heart, utterly conflicted by the rolling beginnings of the orgasm building low inside me, and the prospect of how I will cope with what he's about to do. "Yeah. Yes, I trust you." I exhale, trying to prepare myself.

A deep breath is not enough, though. The burning heat of the pain that lances through me when Zeth pushes slowly into my ass is overwhelming. I grab onto the headboard, handcuffs digging deep into my skin, and I brace myself against the all-consuming sensation. He's not even close to being all the way inside me when he stops, leaning around my body to work the vibrator inside my pussy, his other hand working my clit.

"Relax. Breathe, Sloane." He kisses my shoulder, licking at my skin, growling as I tighten and tense around him. "You say when. You're in control."

I don't feel very in control in my current position, tied to the bed and impaled on his cock, but I know he's not lying to me. I may not feel in control, but I can make this stop at any moment. I can just say the word and it will be over. But…but I don't want it to be over.

Because underneath the pain and the burning heat…it feels good.

"Slowly," I whisper. "Just…go slow."

So he does. Millimeter by millimeter, Zeth carefully begins to rock against me, easing himself inside. With each and every minute movement of his body against mine, my muscles lose their tension. It's not long before I'm moving with him, tilting my hips back, testing out the boundaries of what I can take here.

"Fuck. You're so fucking perfect," Zeth groans. "This is killing me. I just wanna fuck you so hard. Bury my dick inside you 'til my balls are slapping that tight ass of yours."

"Then…then do it." I know I'm going to be living on a knife-edge, regretting and glorying in those words as soon as they've left my mouth, but I still say them.

Zeth lets out a carnal, inarticulate sound as he draws himself out of me and then thrusts back inside. He's shaking, his body vibrating against me as he fucks me. I never thought it would be possible to come like this, but I can feel it building inside me even now. The small pulses of pleasure shooting through me because of the vibrator are intensified a hundredfold by the sound of Zeth's own pleasure firing through him. It pushes me over the edge.

My arms and legs pull in as my orgasm rips through me like a bullet out of a gun. Zeth's fingers dig into my ass, fingernails breaking the skin, as he climaxes at the same time. I can feel him pulsing inside me, filling me, claiming me as his.

Neither of us can breathe, speak, move when it's over. Zeth presses his forehead into my back, fighting to fill his lungs, until I can't bear him inside me anymore and I twist away. I slump down onto the bed, my hands still held up over my head, and Zeth works to free me.

"You think the neighbors heard?" he asks breathlessly.

"Buddy, if I had any neighbors, they'd have called the police on your ass a long time ago." My body feels thoroughly stretched and sore in the best kind of way. I collapse on top of him, my head on his chest, my hand over his heart—it's still galloping inside his ribcage.

"You're gonna have a heart attack one of these days," I muse.

Zeth laughs, stroking one hand up and down my sweat-slick back. "If I do, don't resuscitate me, angry girl. That would be the best fucking way to die."

ZETH

Three weeks later

For the first time in my living memory, Christmas didn't suck major ass this year. And now that New Years' is long gone and everyone's quit singing Silent Night, things are finally getting into a routine. A fucking *routine*. Sounds so stupid, and yet here I am. My favorite part of this routine, after hanging out with Sloane and all that entails, is working at the gym.

If there's one thing I know how to do in this life, it's how to knock someone the fuck out. Michael reels backward as I hammer my fist into his face, blood exploding from his mouth. Pain sings out in my right hand—my knuckles were split open about seven minutes ago. Now they're a royal fucking mess.

My boy rights himself, swiping his blood from his lips, giving me the kind of dark, shitty look I normally reserve for the spineless motherfuckers who come in here trying to spar with me on a Friday night. The t-shirt fillers, wanting to bulk up before they go out on the weekend to impress the women. Wanting to feel like proper badasses by taking down the owner of the gym.

Pity for them I don't go down easy. Or ever, really. I'm betting it's hard for them to feel very masculine with the busted-up noses and the black eyes I hand out, either. Serves them right.

"You call that a hook?" Michael spits blood onto the ground, flexing out his own hands. His white wife beater is stained with his blood and mine, kind of like some weird hippy Rorschach tie-dye. All I see in the patterns our blood makes is guns and explosions. Make of that what you will.

"I nearly put you on your ass, motherfucker," I growl at him. If he's trying to bait me, he won't need to do much to succeed tonight. I haven't fucked Sloane in two days. She's been working nights at the hospital and I've been training early. It's left zero time for me to drive her crazy, or for me to expel some of my pent-up tension. Since I'm no longer working for a gang lord, the extra energy that would have been burned up by the adrenalin firing through my veins as I sped through the streets of Seattle on whatever dark and dangerous mission I'd been commissioned with now sits dormant in the pit of my stomach, gathering momentum. It explodes out of me in these matches I hold with Michael, or any other asshole dumb enough to verse me. Owning a fighting gym, I'm not exactly in short supply of those.

"You look tired. You wanna call it quits?" Michael asks, and even as he says this he's laughing. He knows what his words will do to me.

"Tired?" I clench my hands into fists, lowering my cantering of gravity before putting my guard up and stalking forward. "I don't get tired when it counts, Michael."

"And when does it count?" he laughs, putting up his own fists, rocking from side to side on the balls of his feet. Michael may not be able to hit quite as hard as me, but the guy's quick on his feet. He snaps out punches faster than lightning.

"When I'm fighting and when I'm fucking, of course," I tell him. "Not that you'd know anything about the last part. When was the last time you got laid again?" I feint to the left, bringing home a nasty uppercut with my right hand. It connects with his side, right in the ribcage. His breath wheezes out of him, but his guard stays up. Whoever taught him to fight taught him well.

Yeah, that would be me.

"I got laid last night, boss." Out comes his left fist in a jab. It makes contact with my jaw, snapping my head around. Fucking hurts, but I grin at him. I know my teeth are stained red with blood—I can taste it on my tongue, the copper lighting up my senses. I'm vaguely aware that I must look like some kind of monster.

"Bullshit," I say. "If you used your dick last night, you wouldn't be fighting like such a fucking pussy."

We circle one another, both looking for an in.

"If I'm fighting like a pussy, then I dread to think what kind of pussy you've been getting."

I immediately stop, freezing to the spot. I straighten up, letting my hands drop to my side out of guard. Tipping my head to one side, I shake it at the same time, pinning him in my unblinking gaze. My boy stills himself too, realization dawning on his face. He knows what he's said. And I can clearly see that he wishes he could take it back.

"Fuck, man, I'm sorry. I guess I'm just not used to you having a partner."

I give him a dark look.

"A girlfriend?"

I growl, low and deep in my throat.

"A mistress? Fuck, man, I don't know. I'm sorry. I didn't mean anything by it. You know I love Sloane."

"You're not helping."

Michael holds up his hands. I can see the smile begging to spread across his face, but he's smart enough not to let it happen. "You know what I mean, Zee. I love her like a sister. A white, super tall, ridiculously attractive sister."

I go for him, charging across the ring, ready to pick his ass up and slam it down onto the boards. Michael barks out a single *ha!* of laughter before my body slams into his, driving him backward. We're on the ropes then, and I'm raining down strikes to his torso while he shields his head with his arms. I can still hear him laughing. The bastard is as crazy as me.

"You wanna take that back?"

"Yes! Yeah—ah—fuck!" Michael gasps in between his laughter. "Jesus, man!"

I stop, stepping back, my chest hitching, my breathing fast as I playfully thump him on the arm. "No one gets to talk shit about my girl, Michael. Not even you."

"I think I've got three broken ribs that will attest to that," he says, pulling himself upright. He knows I'm mostly joking. Mostly. I wasn't hitting him anywhere near as hard as I could have, but I know a few of those punches must have rung his bell a little. I smirk at him, assessing how fucked he looks. I'm too busy admiring my handiwork to see the intent in his eyes, before he launches at me with a barrage of his own punches. I can do nothing but duck and shield while he lands a succession of powerful hits to my arms, shoulders, ribcage and the side of my head.

It's not long before I'm laughing, too. The sound must throw Michael—laughter is a relatively new development for me, after all—because he eases back a little. Big mistake. I take the opportunity to go for him again, this time for his legs. I land a solid front kick, right in his stomach. He goes down with a strangled *ufff*, and then I'm straddling him in mount, smashing my fists into him again.

"Fuck me, you guys are insane!"

My head snaps to the side, my right fist frozen in mid-air, Michael's bloody wife beater bunched up in my other hand. Michael stills too, peering out from behind his guard.

There's a kid standing at the side of the ring, chewing on gum, ball cap flipped backward on his head, staring at us like we're fucking insane. I look down at Michael, lifting one eyebrow. "You see what I see?" I ask.

Michael nods. "I sure do."

"And there was me thinking we were closed." I slowly rise to my feet, stepping over Michael and pacing carefully, deliberately toward the intruder. I let every single ounce of malice I can muster radiate through me as I stop in front of the kid. "You wanna tell me how you got in here?" I ask slowly. "Because I fucking *know* I locked up for the night."

The kid has the common sense to look worried. I take him in, assessing him as he shifts from one foot to the other. Clear, open-looking green eyes. He's tall, maybe six-one, six-two. There's a small scar running down the side of his head, from his temple to the curve of his cheekbone. Can't tell what color hair he's got underneath that ball cap but from his eyebrows I'm going with dark brown. Even though he's clearly shitting himself, he holds himself upright and rigid. It's a fighter's stance, if a bad one. I catch sight of his Gracie Barra hoody and I know what that means: he's either a wannabe Ju Jitsu fighter or he just loves watching UFC on TV. "You feel like answering me anytime soon?" I rumble.

"I just wanted to train. I didn't—"

"Break in?"

"Well, yeah, I mean…I *did*." He looks lost, like he's about to bolt any second. Michael comes and stands behind me, giving off an unmistakeable *prepare-to-be-fucked-up* vibe. I push the ropes of the ring down and vault over them, landing right in front of the kid. I'm on the fence. I should be right there with Michael, ready to give this little shit the beating of his life for breaking into my gym, but my curiosity is getting the better of me. "Why didn't you leave when you realized someone was here? Huh? Answer me."

He shrinks back into himself, shrugging his shoulders. "I was watching you guys. You were going to town on each other. People don't spar like they wanna kill each other normally. Guess I was a little fascinated. Wanted to see who would win."

Michael crosses his arms over his chest, still covered in blood, looking formidable. "And what do you think? In your expert opinion, who was winning?"

The kid's eyebrows almost hit his hairline. He doesn't realize he's being fucked with. "I don't know. You both looked pretty even to me. You gonna call the cops or what?"

I know Michael's looking at me, waiting to see how I will react. I know full well how *he* wants to fucking react. He wants to laugh his ass off; I can feel it bubbling off him. I beat him to it, rumbling out my own laughter, right from the bottom of my ribcage. "How old are you?"

The kid looks from me to Michael, like this is some sort of trick question. "Twenty-three."

"Twenty-three?"

"Yeah."

"You got a job?"

Uncertainty flickers across his face again. "Yeah. I work at Mac's." He jerks his head over his shoulder, toward the door.

"Mac's, the auto mechanics across the street?" I've seen the place. They deal in specialty cars. I thought about taking the Camaro over there before I noticed flashy pieces driving through the roller shutters at weird times of the night. Last thing I need is even stepping foot inside a place that cuts and shuts cars or burns VIN numbers off stolen vehicles.

The kid nods. "Yeah. I see you guys training over here sometimes when I'm on my break."

I fit the gym out with a huge roller shutter of its own, so that we could get some airflow in here when we're busy. It stands open during the day, when we're open. "And your name?" I ask. "Better tell me the fucking truth."

"Mason. Mason Reeves." He says it too quickly for it to be a lie.

"All right, Mason, Mason Reeves, if you have a job working over at Mac's and you're earning money, why the hell aren't you paying to come into my gym during daylight hours, huh?" I take a step closer to him, still considering planting my fist in his face. How the next few seconds play out right now all depends on what comes out of this fucker's mouth.

Mason looks me in the eye and shrugs. "I don't have to explain myself to you, man."

"Ah, yeah, actually you do. Otherwise my boy Michael here is going to break something of yours. And it won't be something small like your fingers. It'll be something big. Something that means you won't be working at Mac's for a while, after all."

Michael straightens up at this, as though he's

looking forward to the prospect of physical work. Things have been pretty low key since Charlie died. Michael's been mostly checking in on Sloane to make sure no one's following her. And also running tabs on the DEA. As Liam Neeson would say, though, he has a very particular set of skills, and he likes to use them. Just like me.

Mason lifts his chin, staring at us both. If he's perturbed by the fact that Michael's about to hospitalize him, he's barely showing it. Barely.

"Whatever, man. I don't come during the day because I'm at work."

"There's an all-night gym three blocks that way." I point in the direction of the commercialized gym a five-minute walk down the road, raising my eyebrows. "Try again. This time the truth, motherfucker."

Mason steps forward, a spark of something firing in his eyes. His chin is still lifted, showing me he's not afraid of me. It's a good show, but I can read him like a book. He's freaked, but he won't lose face by backing down. Good for him. Really fucking dumb, but good for him. "I have a sister to take care of," he says. "I have rent to cover, and I gotta get school shit for her. I can't afford expensive gyms."

Michael looks down at his feet, smiling, arms

still crossed. I sigh, not too impressed by the fact that I now feel obliged to *not* beat him up. "Where's your mother?" I realize I sound like a fifty-year-old as I ask this. Fucking ridiculous.

"Dead. Drug overdose. It's just me and my sister. My dad left when I was four. Millie's dad left when my mom died. You want my whole life story, or are you just gonna call the fucking cops, so we can get this over with?"

Well, fuck me, the kid has stones. I get the feeling this isn't the first time he's had to front up to someone much bigger and much scarier than he is. I can appreciate that it takes some form of courage, even if that form of courage is mainly rooted in stupidity. Sloane would call him brave. I call him asking for it.

"I'm not gonna call the cops," I tell him.

"You're not?" He actually looks surprised, like the very sight of me isn't enough to tell him that I'm hardly on the best of terms with local law enforcement.

"Nope. You're gonna get in that ring with me. You can lay a couple of good hits on me, you can come train here *during open hours*."

Steel forms in the kid's eyes. "Why can't it be him?" he says, jerking his head in Michael's direction.

"Ha! I don't know if I should be flattered or offended," Michael says.

"What does it matter who it is? I thought you said we looked pretty even." I smirk because I'm an evil motherfucker and I know, despite how much I respect Michael, that I was winning that fight. I usually do, which is not to say Michael isn't seriously capable with his fists. I'm just more capable.

"And what happens if I *don't* get a couple of good hits on you?"

"Then I probably knock you out and that's the end of it."

"I can go?"

"Sure." I'm feeling very benevolent, even though I shouldn't be. At least I know now that I need to replace the fucking locks.

"Okay, then. Fine." Mason nods, as though he's steeling himself, and then he rips his Gracie Barra hoody over his head. He moves past me to climb into the ring. The guy's not really a kid, after all. He's clearly in shape, arms full of tattoos. He has a fighter's physique. How long has he been training in my fucking gym without me knowing? I can see by the way he's smiling that Michael's thinking the same thing, as I jump back into the ring after Mason.

"You got gloves?" I ask him.

"*You're* not wearing gloves."

I pick up my gloves from the corner of the ring, arching an eyebrow at him. "I doubt you're ready for the bare-knuckle version of me, kid."

I've been fighting like that since I was a teenager, training with Charlie's bagmen and enforcers all throughout my physically formative years. Most people aren't like that, though. Most people have never thrown a punch and felt their actual fist make contact with someone's face. It's not exactly painless.

Michael tosses up his own gloves to Mason, shaking his head as he takes a seat at the edge of the ring, ready to watch this go down. It starts as soon as the kid has his gloves on. I move in, fast and explosive, landing a heavy hit to his side.

Mason absorbs the blow, wincing only a little as he adjusts his guard. He's light on his feet like Michael, but I can also see immediately that he hasn't benefitted from the same training. His guard is sloppy. There are so many gaps for me to get through, it's not even funny. I point this out by jabbing my fist directly through his hands and smacking him squarely on the forehead. It's not an actual hit. It's me showing him how open he's leaving himself.

We go on like this for a full minute. I see an

opening. I take it. I prod or jab him. I show him all the ways I could hurt him, but I don't. Mason just takes it. He stares solidly at me, wheeling around, trying to get away from me where he can. It's the third time I jab him on his forehead that he gets tired of the abuse and counters.

I can see the moment where he decides enough is enough. I know what's going through his head: *It'd be better to have him actually retaliating and hitting me properly than to be mocked.* He comes at me, sending punch after punch, fast, with a good rhythm, until I find myself taking a step back. One step.

"Boss, if you still want to collect your better half, it's time we finished things up here," Michael says.

That's all I need to hear. I dodge one of Mason's more powerful punches, pivoting my body to the right so that I have a clear shot at his open side, and then I hit him. I really hit him. He doubles over, and I bring my left fist up in an uppercut that sends him reeling. I didn't hit him anywhere near as hard as I could, if I'd set my mind to it. I hit him hard enough for him to *remember* it.

He goes down.

He doesn't get back up again for six seconds. That's a hell of a long time to be on the ground if you're fighting someone. The kid's eyes are flashing with disappointment and fury when he faces me again. "I thought you were gonna knock me out," he says.

"Not this time. Maybe I will next time, though."

"What next time?"

I take my gloves off and toss them on the boards, shaking my head. I can't believe I'm even about to fucking say this. "The next time you come in here. During open hours. We'll train again then. But if I find out you've been in here again when I'm not, I'll skin you alive, motherfucker, you read me?"

Mason ducks his head, then stoops and collects his hoody. He puts it back on and then fixes me in that weird, challenging stare of his. Has nobody told him he's not fucking Al Capone yet? "All right," he says. "Thanks, man. I guess I'll see you tomorrow, then." He vaults over the ropes and that's it. He leaves without looking back once.

"You know you're turning into a soft fucking touch, don't you?" Michael says, slinging me my own zip-up hoody.

I glare at him, but we both know I don't mean it. "Keep saying stuff like that and I'll have to prove you wrong, asshole."

As we leave the gym and I make sure everything is locked up tight, pointless though that now seems, Michael digs me in the side. "Seriously, though, man. A year ago someone would have found that kid unconscious in the gutter out here. And now you're gonna train him?"

I sigh, scratching at my jaw. There are two reasons why I did what I did, but I can only tell Michael one of them. "He didn't back down. He didn't give up. He had enough fire in him to force me back a step, too. That's something. Maybe there's more."

"Maybe." Michael tosses me the keys to the Camaro, and I climb into the driver's seat, slamming the door behind me. He remains silent on the drive over to St. Peter's Hospital—the guy just knows when he should talk and when he shouldn't —and I use the quiet to gather my thoughts. Yeah, I did let the kid get away with breaking into the gym because I can see some sort of potential in him. But I also let him get away with it because the way he looked at me, so fierce and determined yet downtrodden at the same time, reminded me of someone.

Someone we buried next to a river in the mountains.

SLOANE

I feel the tear widening even as I desperately try to pack the open cavity in front of me. Shit.

Fuck, shit, motherfucker.

The guy on my operating table is eighteen years old, and he's been suffering from bowel cancer since he was thirteen. I'm not even his regular doctor. Since I came back to work, I've been making headway in the trauma department, forging a serious name for myself. I was always steady before, but now, after spending so much time with Zeth, dealing with psychotic mob bosses, human traffickers, and DEA agents, it's like I'm bomb proof. Unshakable. People have started noticing, especially the chief.

So when Miles Rosenblat, eighteen, was rushed into the emergency room an hour ago complaining of severe stomach pains and Dr Wishall, his oncologist, wasn't on shift, I was handed his patient and told to save his life.

"His father donates a huge amount of money to this hospital, Dr. Romera. Better not let his son die on your table," were the chief's exact words, in fact.

At this point, I'm not so sure I'll be able to accomplish that. The kid's bowels are a mess. He was supposed to be in remission, but it's very clear that the cancer snuck back in and made itself right at home while no one was looking. His colon has just torn so badly there's no way I'm going to be able to repair it. Best case scenario: I'm gonna be giving this kid a colostomy before I can close him up and his life changes forever. Worst case scenario: I give him the colostomy, close him up, he gets an infection, and then he dies in a couple of days' time.

Either way, it's not the bright and shiny outcome the chief's waiting on up in the observatory. I'm sure she can see what I'm dealing with though.

Oliver Massey, my closest friend at the hospital, leans over the patient's body and shakes his head. "Fuck."

"Yeah. My thoughts exactly."

"There's too much to resect. You'll have to take the whole thing."

"I know." I'm working quickly as I say this, already preparing to remove all of the damaged, necrotic tissue. Some doctors might be irritated by being told something so obvious by their colleagues, but I don't mind Oliver giving his opinion. It makes me feel better about the decision I've made.

For the next three hours we work tirelessly over Miles, doing our best to remove anything that might be even faintly cancerous. When we're done, Miles Rosenblat has a brand new stoma. He's a fit, good looking kid with a perky blonde girlfriend waiting for him out in the hallway. I already know he is going to *hate* having a stoma.

"Poor bastard," Oliver says, ripping off his gown and tossing into the HAZMAT as we clear the OR. "I think the chief said he's on his high school football team. Football jocks are assholes when it comes to this sort of thing."

I scrub my hands over my face, my eyes stinging and tired from concentrating so hard. "But he's alive."

Oliver pulls a cautiously optimistic face. He knows Miles isn't out of the woods yet. Not by a long shot. He doesn't say anything, though. He knows I don't want to hear it right now. Instead, he says, "Damn. It's ten thirty. You wanna grab a beer before all the bars shut?"

My stomach rolls when I hear the time. Oh, boy. Zeth knew my shift was ending at eight. He was coming to get me. He's either been waiting for me in the parking lot for two and a half hours or he's already left. Neither of those options are good. "Ahh, crap. I can't tonight, Ol. Maybe tomorrow?"

Oliver doesn't even look surprised. I've bailed on him more times than I can count over the past few months. I'm a terrible friend. "Sure, Romera. Tomorrow it is. I'll just head on over and pay Grace a visit instead." He winks, leaving no doubt as to why he's going over to see some girl called Grace. He holds the door to the residents' locker room open for me, and I duck inside.

"Who's Grace? What happened to Melanie?"

"Melanie decided she wanted to get married.

Grace is happy for me to come over whenever we both feel the need to release some tension." Another wink. Obviously code for sex.

"What? Melanie did *not* want to get married. You guys were dating for, what, six weeks?"

"Seven. And she wanted to introduce me to her parents. That's what chicks do when they wanna get married."

I stifle laughter as I remove my dirty scrubs, shrugging out of my shirt and kicking out of my pants. I bundle everything up so I can dump it in yet another HAZMAT bin. In just my camisole and the lycra shorts I wear underneath my scrubs, I place my hands on my hips, facing Oliver. "I never had you pegged as a player. Here was me thinking you wanted a steady girlfriend. You used to talk about that all the time."

Oliver smirks, stripping off his own scrubs to reveal a tight white wife beater underneath. He's gotten bigger over the last six months. He has always worked out, but now he looks like he could be a fitness model or something. Clearly all of his random five-minute hook-ups have kept him in shape. "Yeah, well," he says, rummaging in his locker. "Things change. The girl I was interested in having a proper relationship with went and got herself attached to someone else, didn't she?" He doesn't look at me. Taking out a clean tshirt, he pulls it on over his head, not saying anything else.

My cheeks feel like they're on fire. Oliver's always treated me as a friend, but I've known he cared about me for a long time. Recently things have been different, though. Used to be that he'd give me the odd playful shove or pull on my hair when we were walking through the hallways. There were many times when he'd give me a hug after I'd lost someone, or I was gripped by panic over my missing sister. But not now. Not anymore. As I get dressed, pulling jeans and a sweater on, it hits me that he's avoided all forms of physical contact with me for a long time now.

Sadness wells up inside me, making my throat tight. I don't have feelings for Oliver; I never have. Yet, the change in our dynamic is saddening. I feel like he's pulling back as a friend, which is ridiculous since I'm the one turning him down every time he asks to hang out. I guess with Zeth being, well, *Zeth*, I haven't wanted a moment away from him. Being in his very presence is like a drug I can't get enough of. Is that healthy? I can't remember the last time I saw Pippa. Maybe three weeks ago when we caught up for coffee at Fresco's?

"Oliver, I mean it. I really do want to go for a

drink with you after work tomorrow. You think you can skip Grace for one night?"

Oliver gives me a tight smile, swinging his backpack onto his shoulder. "Of course, Romera. I'll make time for you whenever you need me, you know that." He makes a gun out of his right hand and fires it at me. If only he knew how many times I've had the real thing pointed at me. "I'll see you in the morning, yeah?" he says.

"Yeah. Night, Oliver."

I check my phone as soon as he's gone. I have one missed call and one text message, both from Zeth. The call came in at eight thirty. The text fifteen minutes later. *I hear you're wrist-deep in some kid or something.*

Come home soon so I can be balls deep inside you.

I shouldn't be turned on by such a blatant text, but I am. Sue me. The idea of Zeth inside me right now is enough to make me shiver in anticipation. After the stress of such a huge surgery, I need to unwind, and there is no better way to do that than to let my boyfriend have his dark, deviant way with me.

I grab my stuff and hurry out of the hospital before I can get caught up in any new patients, wondering if there will be any taxis available at this time of night. I don't get four feet out of the building before I realize I won't need one, though. Michael's black sedan is parked right next to the entrance. *Of course, I should have known.* The driver's door opens and Michael climbs out, smoothing his hands down the front of his pristine grey suit. The man is always so well turned out. Today, however, his look is ruined by the fact that he's sporting a black eye and a nasty split lip. "What the hell happened to you?"

He shrugs, smiling. "Ask your boyfriend."

"Oh god, he didn't try and kill you, did he?"

"Only a little." Michael opens the passenger door for me and then climbs back into the car himself. As he drives, heading in the direction of our house on the hill as Zeth calls it, I prod my finger at the gash I can now see on the side of his head.

"You guys are really gonna hurt each other one of these days."

"Probably."

"Why did he make you wait for me? Has something happened?" You never know what's around the corner when you're dating a guy like Zeth Mayfair. Seems as though trouble follows him around like a bad smell. I'm used to the concept that people don't like him living here in Seattle. Criminals all over the city know exactly who he is and what he's capable of. According to Michael, no one can really believe he's retired from the life. They're just waiting for him to step up and claim what they presume is rightly his.

"No, everything's fine," Michael says. "He told me to go home, that you'd be okay, but I had to go see someone anyway. I was passing by here and thought I'd check in on you."

"You had to see someone, huh?" I let my amusement color my voice. I've had a sneaking suspicion Michael has been seeing someone for a while now, but he's a private guy. He hasn't cracked, even under the most intense questioning. I guess, amongst other, more violent reasons, that's why Zeth likes to keep him around.

"It was business," he says, biting back a smile.

"Yeah. I bet it was."

"Seriously."

"I bet it was dirty business."

"Which involves?"

"Your penis. And paddles. Maybe a hard-core dominatrix called Madame Payne. And probably a lot of sweat."

"I think you're confusing my sex life with yours."

"Are you calling Zeth a hard-core dominatrix?"

"Not within earshot."

I laugh, not pushing him any further. One of these days he'll tell me. Or maybe he won't. Maybe there's always going to be a side to Michael I don't know. I doubt he tells Zeth anything either.

We drive in comfortable silence up the winding roads that lead to the house; when we pull up outside, the place is dark, not a single light on inside. I can already hear the rhythmic thwack, thwack, thwack that tells me my antsy other half is out the back, indulging in his favorite pastime while I'm not around. I sigh, leaning across the car to give Michael a swift kiss on the cheek. "Thank you for bringing me home."

"No problem. Have a good night, Ms. Romera."

I wish he would call me Sloane. No matter how many times I tell him, it never seems to stick. Instead of letting myself inside the house, I skirt around the side, heading for the woods out back. He's there, shirtless and sweating, a gas lamp burning at his feet, as he brings up the ax in his hands and swings it down onto the block of wood in front of him.

I don't even have an open fire. Zeth just likes hitting things with axes.

"There she is," he rumbles. I've been silent as a mouse, but of course he knows I'm behind him. He rests the ax head on the ground, angling his head toward me. I'm a hopeless case. No matter how many times I see this man partially undressed, I can't help but stare at him. He's so perfect. His body is perfection. The sweat-slicked muscles in his back shift ever so slightly as he leans his weight to one side, waiting for me to reach him. If I were capable of controlling myself around him, I would maybe kiss him lightly on the mouth in greeting and ask him what he's been doing all day. The embarrassing thing is that I'm not capable of controlling myself around him, though. I find myself slowly licking the groove in between his shoulder blades, my tongue exploding with the taste of the salt in his sweat, my hands itching to touch him as he rocks his head back and groans.

"I liked your text message," I whisper.

"Thought you might." Zeth spins around grabs hold of me before I have a chance to say anything else. I like being tall, but I also love the way Zeth makes me feel small when he takes hold of me. Small and protected. Completely overpowered. Giving myself over to him, so that he knows he has dominion over me, wasn't an easy task, but when he grabs hold of me like this and makes me feel like I'm his, now I feel complete. He wraps his strong arms around me and growls into the curve of skin where my neck meets my collarbone.

"You smell like sin," he whispers.

"Mmm?"

"You want me. I can fucking smell it on you." He nips me with his teeth, hard enough to make me gasp.

"Maybe I do."

"You want me to fuck you, angry girl? 'Cause I'm not opposed to the idea. And neither is my dick." His hot breath sends searing vibrations shooting through my body. The sound I make in the back of my throat is loud and embarrassing, but it seems to spur Zeth on. His hands work their way underneath my sweater, his fingers skating over the skin of my belly, up, up, up until he reaches the swell of my breast.

"You have to say it, Sloane. I want to hear you tell me how badly you want me."

"I *do* want you. I need you. I need you inside me.

Please…"

Zeth traces the line of my jaw with his free hand, and then he tilts my head back with his thumb, so that I'm looking up into his dark, fierce eyes. "Are you going to do what I tell you to?" he asks. "Because I need you to be a good girl for me, Sloane."

He brushes his thumb over my bottom lip, staring at my mouth. He constantly surprises me with what dark, sexual things run through his head. I can never guess what he's thinking. If he were another guy, I'd assume he was thinking about me wrapping my mouth around his cock right now, but it's never that simple with Zeth. He's complicated in his desires. A small frown flickers across that savagely beautiful face of his. Pain rockets through me as he pinches and rolls my nipple through the thin lace of my bra.

"You haven't answered me, Sloane. Are you going to do what I tell you?"

"Yes. Yes, I'll do what you tell me." Two days. We haven't slept with each other in two days, and it's just too long. I've been wanting him, needing him, fantasizing about him every moment I haven't been focused on saving someone's life. And I'm betting he's been focused on all the things he wants to do to me too, especially while he's been smashing his fist into things.

Zeth leans forward and bites my lower lip, hard, still pinching my nipple. I suck in a sharp breath, letting the bright sensation of pain cascade through me. He stops biting me, but runs his tongue over my lip instead, tasting me in that highly sexual way he has. The way he licks at my mouth is the same way he licks at my clitoris when he first goes down on me—slow and drawn out. His eyes are locked onto mine, burning and intense, and I can't help the strangled noise that comes out of me.

"Fuck, Zeth."

He instantly stops what he's doing, removing himself from me, taking a step back. My nipple throbs with the ache that he's left behind, begging for more of the same. There was a time when I would have shied away from the strange urge to let him own me, to let him have complete power over me, but not anymore. Now, I crave it in the same way my body craves oxygen.

No one else knows this side of me. My friends, my family my work colleagues…everyone knows the strong, resilient, commanding Sloane. They would never imagine me to be like this with anyone. But being strong, resilient and commanding at all times is exhausting, especially when I feel like I'm making things up as I go along most days. Zeth takes the pressure of being me of my shoulders when he owns me like this. He gives me permission to be vulnerable.

The night air teases at the loose strands of hair that have fallen out of my ponytail, as I stand completely still. Zeth stalks around me, looking me up and down with hungry eyes. I can see the goose bumps on his shoulders, and I know it's not because it's cold. It's because he's turned on and he's thinking about what he's going to do to me.

He circles me once, twice, and I resist the urge to reach out and touch him. My hands stay by my sides, though it takes everything I've got to hold back. He stops behind me, close enough that I can feel his hot breath on the back of my neck. "Take your clothes off for me, Sloane. I want to watch."

My breathing stutters out of me in one long, broken sigh. Zeth circles me one last time before he takes a seat on the tree stump he was using as a base to chop the wood on. Even though he's only five feet away, he still doesn't feel close enough. I want his hands on my body again. I want to feel him growing more and more impatient as he teases his fingers across my burning skin. I know I won't get any of that until I've done what he wants me to do, though.

I start with my sweater. It's warm enough in Seattle right now to not need a coat. I don't have anything on under the sweater, either, so when I slowly, carefully lift it over my head, I'm left standing there in nothing but my bra.

Zeth's eyelids lower a little, looking heavy as he

watches me. The power of his gaze on my skin is enough to put fire in my veins. I love the way he looks at me. Love the way his eyes travel over my body like he's imagining consuming me in the most erotic ways possible.

I kick off my shoes, not caring that the grass is slightly damp on my bare feet. My jeans are next. I don't even attempt to make a show out of it. I'd end up

tripping over my own pants, and besides, trying to put on a striptease for him would look porny and fake. That's not what he wants. He just wants to see *me*. I can't tear my eyes off him as he watches my hands move over my body, removing my clothes one piece at a time. He looks fascinated by the process. I'm not even mildly embarrassed as I slip out of my bra and panties. I feel liberated. I feel alive. My body aches for him as he considers me, lit only by the soft glow of the gas lamp that sits on the ground between us.

"You're so fucking perfect," he whispers. "Come here."

I go to him, and he opens his legs so I can stand between them. Carefully, reverently, he raises his right hand and strokes his fingers across my stomach, coming to rest on my hip. His hands aren't soft. They've been used to fight his whole life. He's built so many things for the gym and for the house in the last few months, and he's chopped about three truckloads of wood just for fun. They're calloused and rough, but the way he uses them to touch me is so very gentle.

With him still sitting down, he has to look up at me as he touches me. His left hand moves up my body, palming the heavy swell of my breast, one at a time; he straightens so that he can take the nipple he was pinching a moment ago into his mouth. He may have been staring at my lips not to long ago, but now it's my turn to stare. His lips are incredible. Full and expressive and bitable. I'm already wet, but watching him lick and suck at me while his strong, demanding hands work their way over every part of my skin makes my body go wild.

I can't touch him. I know I can't, not yet, but I want to so badly, it's killing me.

"Your body was made for me, Sloane," he groans. "Turn around."

I know better than to disobey. I'm still a girl, though. I still have my body hang-ups, and my ass is one of them. No one could ever accuse me of not having one, that's for sure. With anyone else, I'd undoubtedly be self-conscious, but my brain is too crowded to even comprehend that right now. I just want to feel him touching me, enjoying me, exploring me. The way he worships my body, from the very first time we slept together, has always made me feel like I *am* perfect.

Zeth runs his hands up over the curve of my ass and then over my hips, taking hold of me so he can pull me back toward him. I feel his mouth, hot and insistent pressing into the skin of my lower back, and then even hotter when he uses his tongue. He travels down, licking and biting at my butt cheek, making me squirm.

"Open your legs, Sloane." His voice is thick with lust, low and demanding. I open my legs, only slightly mortified that he's about to discover what he's done to me. His fingers trail painfully slowly up the inside of my thigh, until he eventually reaches the junction between my legs. He hovers just to the side of my pussy, knowing that it's driving me absolutely insane to have him so close to touching me, and yet refraining. I'm panting, and my legs feel weak. The bastard knows exactly what he's doing to me, and I could wring his neck for it, but I'm also enjoying it. Enjoying it way, *way* too much. This is part of our game. I can't react. I can't just jump him. If I do, he'll torture me until I can't bear it anymore. Sometimes that can be fun, but right now I need him so badly. My body needs to feel like it's complete.

I hold my breath, careful not to move as he bites at me some more, on my hips, my ass, my thigh. The biting gets progressively harder, until I can barely stand anymore. It hurts, yes, but it also feels incredible. Zeth laughs mercilessly under his breath as my own kicks up a notch. Eventually he guides his fingers backward between my legs, sweeping them over my slick pussy, making my whole body lock up. His fingers…his fingers *there*…

I can barely form a coherent thought.

"My god, Sloane," he sighs. "Look at you. You're ready for me, aren't you?"

I look back at him over my shoulder, my heart burning in my chest when I see the awe on his face. He looks almost stunned. I nod, feeling my cheeks burn that little bit hotter. "I need to wrap myself around you," I whisper. "I need you inside me. I need you to hold onto me so tight I can't breathe. I don't want to know where you end and I start anymore."

Zeth makes a guttural, sexual noise that sends chills through my body. It's thrilling. "Lay down on the grass, Sloane." His tone is soft, but it brooks no argument. I know there'll be hell to pay if I object.

The grass is cold and tickles my skin, but my whole body is hypersensitive right now. It feels incredible. Zeth stands up, towering over me, every muscle in his body tensed. The tattoos, the black sweeping ink he's worn for as long as I've known him, look stark against his skin in the half-light. The fleur de lis over his right pec rises and falls quickly along with his chest as he fights to control his breathing.

"Open your legs for me," he commands.

I open them, my nipples hardening to painful buds as he drops to his knees. "You're so wet for me, angry girl. That's all for me. Now I'm going to claim it." He drops to his knees and immediately falls between my legs, groaning as he licks at my pussy, licking me clean. Just as he said he would, he claims every single last drop of my moisture between my legs, replacing it with his saliva. My body reacts explosively. He is so good with his tongue. I feel like I'm going to pass out as he teases his mouth over me time and time again, slowly licking at first and then sucking, speeding up until I'm shamelessly rocking my hips against his face, begging him to let me come. It's not until he slides his fingers inside me that I really lose it. I hitch my legs up, crushing my thighs around his head, barely aware of my surroundings as he fucks me with his fingers and his tongue.

When I come, I scream silently, unable to even make a sound. The intensity of the orgasm rips through me, my back arching off the ground as Zeth continues, regardless of the fact that my entire body is close to breaking point.

The sensation becomes too much. "Stop, stop, stop, fuck, please, stop," I pant.

Zeth carefully withdraws his fingers, but he doesn't remove his mouth. His movements become less demanding, though. When he runs his tongue over me, gently circling the swollen bundle of nerve endings there, it feels more affectionate than anything else. He's not trying to bring me to another orgasm—I doubt I could take that right now. It's more like he's soothing me, and it feels wonderful.

When he does finally pull back, sitting on his heels, he takes his fingers into his mouth and sucks them clean. "It's fucking criminal how good you taste," he says.

I twist onto my side, wanting to hide, mortification catching up with me at last, but he takes hold of my hip and pushes me so that I'm on my back again. With one hand on either side of my head, he braces himself over me, staring own into my eyes. "Don't you fucking hide from me. Don't you fucking dare," he whispers. "You're amazing."

I say the only thing I can think of that seems appropriate in this moment. The words come out nervously, barely audible. "I love you, Zeth. God, I love you so much."

I can see the light from the gas lamp reflected in those deep brown, soulful, angry, wounded eyes of his. He told me that he loved me a while ago, and it's been enough. He's said it a couple of times since, but not very often. Most women would be freaked out by that fact, but I know how hard it was for him to admit it to me in the first place. He's a thing of chaos, a thing of destruction. Chaos and ruin were the only things he knew for so long. It's taking him time to move past that. Pressing his forehead against mine, he closes his eyes and nods slowly.

"Thank you," he whispers.

Again, this might not be what a girl wants to hear when she tells a guy she's in love with him, but the emotion on his face is clear. His thank you is filled with relief. Filled with love. Filled with so much hope and gratitude and sincerity that it takes my breath away all over again.

He says it like me loving him is the most precious gift anyone has ever given to him.

6

MASON

I wake up to crying. Of course I do. Every night, it's the same. Covered in my own sweat, I charge blindly from my bedroom out into the hallway and into the room down the hall, my heart hammering in my chest.

Millie's on the floor already, her tiny body bowed so badly it looks like her spine is about to break. I stop myself from grabbing her up and holding her to me. Instead, I lace my fingers around the back of my head and press my face in the chipped paintwork of the wall beside me, trying not to scream through my clenched teeth.

Fuck. This is so fucking fucked. Mil's heels begin to kick against the bare floorboards as the seizure worsens. Her eyes are rolled back into her head, her jaw clenched tight as he body spasms over and over again. I want to smash my fist into the wall. I feel fucking useless. There's nothing I can do to help her until the fitting stops, so I just have to stand here and wait like an evil son of a bitch while my five-year-old sister goes through this again. *Again.*

I sink down into a crouch, covering my mouth with my hands, just watching her, waiting for the moment, the very *instant* she stills so I can go to her. The seizure lasts for two more minutes, which is a long fucking time. I'm lifting her into my arms, cradling her to me as soon as it's done. She starts crying, tiny little breathless sobs, her small hands curling into my t-shirt, and I feel warmth spreading over my legs as she pisses herself.

Fuck.

"I'm—I'm sss—sorry, Mase. I'm ss—sorry."

"Oh, god." I feel like my heart's being ripped up through my chest and out through my fucking mouth. Holding her closer to me, I stand up and carry her into the bathroom. "Don't be sorry, little mouse. Don't worry about a thing. Here, c'mon, hop into the bath real quick. We'll get you cleaned up and then you can go back to sleep, okay?"

This is our nightly ritual. I wish we had a fucking shower; it takes the bath so long to fill with the water barely dribbling out and the pipes *thunk, thunk, thunk*ing away, and poor Millie standing in her piss-soaked PJs, looking like she's about to cry some more. She rubs at her eyes, tired and sore from fitting, and all I want to do is pick her up and walk out of this shithole. Take her somewhere clean and fucking nice. Have enough money to get her on the books with a proper fucking doctor, who will look at her as an individual and not just another kid living below the poverty line who can't be helped.

I jam the plug into the plughole and collapse onto the cracked tiles, and then I pull my sister's tiny form into me, not caring about the pee. I hold onto her until there's enough water in the tub for her to wash without her freezing her ass off.

Winter was bad. Going through this on a nightly basis with the place so frigid we could see our breath hanging in the air was seriously something I never want to go through again. I've promised myself, fucking *promised*, that next winter me and little Millie will be in a place that at least has fucking heating.

I don't care if I have to sell the car; I'll carry her three miles to school every morning if I have to. I don't care that I have to wear shitty clothes, covered in grease and dirt from work, and I don't care if we don't have a TV. I don't give a shit about drinking with my friends, or going to the fucking movies. All I want is for Millie to be safe and clean and happy. There has to be a fucking way to make that happen. I refuse to let her down the same way our mother did.

I'm not perfect at this, but I'm trying so fucking hard. The last thing I ever expected as a twenty-three-year-old was to be taking care of my little sister. She's quiet as I bathe her. She's always quiet, like she's afraid to fucking speak or move or do something wrong. She's all skinny arms and skinny legs; she's gonna be tall like me eventually, but right now she's just a skinny, underfed kid who needs proper parents, and all she's got is me.

I carry her back to her room and put her in fresh PJs, and I sit with her until she falls asleep again. The seizures are exhausting for her. She never has problems going back to sleep. Seems that's all she does. The meds they have her on rob her of all her energy, turning a six-year-old little girl into a zombie, sleepwalking through a life that's meant to filled with toy ponies and hair braiding, and I don't fucking know what else. But not this. Not meds and pain and midnight baths and crying. It fucking kills me.

I sit with my head in my hands while I run myself a much colder bath so we don't have to fork out for the hot water, and then I lay in the tepid water until it's freezing cold and I'm shivering, my side aching from where that guy at the gym pummelled me.

The alarm clock on my bedside table reads three-forty when I climb back into bed. Three hours. I'm gonna get three hours sleep before I have to get up and drive Millie to school.

That's more than I usually get.

"You're late, asshole."

Mac's bent over a Firebird that must have been brought in last night when I arrive to work. I'm eight minutes late. I don't even bother trying to explain how difficult it is to get a small child up and ready for school, or what a nightmare it is to drive across town in rush hour. Mac doesn't give a shit. All he cares about is that I'm here for work on time, and if I'm not—frequently the case—then he reams me out about it.

"Sorry, Mac."

"*Sorry, Mac?*" He looks up from the engine block, wrench in hand, face full of grease, and frowns at me. "Sorry, Mac ain't gonna cut it much longer, kid. Sooner or later, I'll be finding someone else to take your place, you hear me?" He points the wrench at me, and I feel like ripping it out of his fucking hand and smashing it into his face.

"I know. I'm sorry. I'll work something out." I've been saying the same thing for a while now.

"I don't get it," Mac says, returning to his work. "You should just hire a child minder or some shit to take your kid sister to school. That's what I did with my kids."

"I can't afford a child minder." He knows this well enough. He's the one who pays my meager weekly pay-check. This is just how Mac likes to start the conversation with me. *The* conversation. The one where he tries to get me running cars for him.

"Well, you know there's always extra work here for you if you need it, Mase. Just say the word."

If it were just me and I wanted to make some extra money, I wouldn't have a problem saying yes to his repeated offer.

But Millie…

If I got busted by the cops, there would be no one to take care of her. Even if I didn't get sent down, Child Protection Services would deem me an unfit guardian and take her away. She'd grow up in the care system, passed from pillar to post. Probably get caught up in drugs just like my mother did. I can't do that to her.

"Yeah, man. I'll let you know," I tell Mac, but he and I both know I won't. Mac doesn't like the fact that I work here and I know about all the shit that goes down after dark, and yet I'm not involved. Makes him nervous.

I work my ass off for the rest of the day, fitting out three cars before close of business to try and get back in the boss's good books. I haven't even stopped to eat by the time five o'clock rolls around.

I may not be able to afford a child minder, but I am lucky enough to have a great neighbor who brings Millie home from school with her own kids, and takes care of her until I get home from work. Wanda's a godsend. Without her, I'd be fucked. I shouldn't really take advantage of her kindness. I should head straight home and pick up Mil, but when I walk out of work the very first thing I see is the gym. Blood & Roses. Weird fucking name for a gym, if you ask me. The shutters are up, the lights still on in the back, and I can hear the familiar sound of guys fucking up each others' shit.

I was so surprised when that guy didn't hand me my ass the other night. I thought for sure I was dead; he looked like a UFC fighter, for fuck's sake. And he sure as hell didn't look like a *nice* one. Two nights a week for the past month, I've been picking the lock over there. Only when Wanda could look after Millie late into the evening, which was never for long. But now, maybe I could spend half an hour after work training there every night. Wanda probably wouldn't mind that.

Working out's never been top on my list of priorities, but when my best friend Ben started earning big money in the fighting scene, it got me to thinking. If I can get good, if I can get strong, if I can get an in, I could be earning good money, too.

I shoot Wanda a text to make sure she's okay with the kid for a little while longer, and she replies almost immediately, telling me to bring her some milk on the way home and we'll call it even. And then I'm walking across the road, walking straight into the gym, and walking straight into the guy who could have kicked my ass the other night.

"Whoa, man. Sorry," I say, backing up a step. It's like he was waiting there for me in the shadows, ready to fucking pounce.

He doesn't say anything about the fact that I almost crashed into him. He does pierce me with a very appraising glare, though. "Must be weird walking through the door when it's already open, huh?" he says. His voice sounds like it's coming up from somewhere around his goddamn boots. Vin Diesel's got nothing on this guy.

"Yeah, a little." I attempt a smile, but it feels all wrong with him staring at me like that. I feel like I should be groveling or something. Shame my pride won't ever let me do that. "So…you said I could train here, remember? With you?"

"Oh, I remember." He doesn't say anything else. Just stands there with his arms folded across his chest, his freakishly large muscles bulging out of the long-sleeved black shirt he's wearing. He keeps staring at me; it's starting to make me sweat.

"If you're busy, I can come—"

"Oh, I'm not busy," he says, with a grim, down-turned smile on his face. "Come with me." Turning, he stalks off through the gym, apparently oblivious to the looks he's given as he passes people sparring or just working out. Every last guy in the place follows him with their eyes like he's some kind of fucking god. They watch him until he reaches a metal stairway, jogs up them and disappears through a lit doorway at the top. I stand at the bottom, wondering whether I'm supposed to follow him. That question is answered when he appears in the doorway again, and leans against the doorjamb. "Come the fuck on, Mason Reeves. You expecting me to carry you over the fucking threshold or what?"

I rush up the stairs, kicking myself for not just following him straight up. Now I look like a dick. Perfect. I find myself in a small, incredibly neat office. The huge guy with the muscles pulls out a chair from behind his desk and places it right in front of me. "Sit down."

"What? Why?"

He glowers at me, and the hairs on the back of my neck stand on end. I get the urge to turn around and run back down the stairs, but I don't. I can't. I can't ever turn my back on a problem. That's exactly what this guy could be to me, it seems. "Just. Fucking. Sit. Down," he growls.

I grimace, but I do as I'm told. The guy walks around me and faces me, arms crossed again. "You into drugs?" he asks.

"No."

"You steal shit?" "No."

He crouches down in front of me so we're at the same eye level. "*You run cars?*" By the way he asks, he knows exactly what goes on across the road at Mac's place.

I look him right in the eye and firmly say, "*No.*"

He stares at me some more, probably trying to work out if I'm lying. After a second he straightens up and starts pacing the room. "You involved with the Italians? The Russians?"

I know about the Italians. A couple of brothers from out east, expanding their business, raising some hell here and there. The Russians, I know nothing about. I shake my head, letting him know I don't work for either group.

The guy assesses me some more. The way it feels like he can see straight through me is more than a little unnerving. "You about to ask me out on a date or something?" I snap.

"Watch your fucking mouth. You wanna walk down those stairs in a moment or you want your ass thrown down them?"

I refuse to answer him. Instead, I just fix my gaze on the wall, clenching my jaw. The guy paces again, and I avoid looking at him.

"My name is Zeth. Like I said yesterday, you can come here and train with me a couple of times a week. But you step outta line fucking once, and you're gone. You hear me?"

I suddenly feel really goddamn sick. Zeth? I may not know a great deal about the organised crime in this town, but I sure as hell know that name. Mac used to have to pay dues to Charlie Holsan before he died. Nearly twenty percent of his profit from both his legit and illegal businesses went into that crazy English bastard's back pocket. News spread like wild fire when he was killed, and there was one name on everyone's lips: Zeth Mayfair.

Mac closed the shop early the day he heard. He bought three bottles of Johnny Blue and kept pouring shots for his employees until every single one of those bottles was empty. Each time he lifted that shot glass to his mouth, the toast went to Zeth Mayfair. Does Mac have any idea that the guy who nearly gave him alcohol poisoning runs the gym over here? Fuck knows. I sure as shit ain't gonna tell him.

I can't believe I broke into his fucking gym. No wonder the guys down on the floor all look at him that way. The guy's notorious.

"I said," Zeth ducks down in front of me, "*do you hear me, asshole?*"

"Yeah. Yeah, of course, man. I won't step out of line, I swear." *Not now I know who you are, anyway. I'm not fucking retarded.*

"All right. Go down to the lockers and grab a pair of gloves and a head guard. Mauy Thai today. Wait for me by the cage. I have a phone call to make."

It was one thing being in a ring with this guy when I didn't have a clue who he was, but now that I know he's a stone-cold psycho and he wants to shut me in a *cage* with him, I'm having second thoughts. He can probably feel my hesitation pouring off me. "You don't want to, that's fine by me. Go hit a speed bag for forty minutes on your own, see what you learn. Either way, get the fuck out of here so I can make my phone call."

He doesn't need to tell me twice. I'm up out of the chair and jogging down the stairs before he can blink. The door to his office slams closed behind me, and I feel a bead of sweat run down between my shoulder blades. Jesus Christ. I should get out of here before he comes down, and I should *not* fucking come back. The guys training around me shoot me curious looks, as though they weren't really expecting me to make it back down here again. I shake my head as I pass them, counting myself lucky that I did. I should just go home and grab Millie. I can figure out another way to train for the fights without the risk of associating myself with a guy like Zeth fucking Mayfair. But even as I'm hurrying across the gym floor in a direct beeline for the exit, my mind is already racing. What other option do I have to train? Especially an option that's as good as this? I mean, training with him? That's like being trained by De Silva or something. He might be crazy and he might have killed the worst mob boss Seattle has ever seen, but that also means he's the best. Where else would I get training like that? And for free?

I know, even as I'm slowing down, that I'm not gonna make it to the exit. The sigh that works its way out from deep inside my chest feels like resignation, tinged with a little panic. This could go bad for me. This could go really fucking bad. As I make a course correction, reluctantly heading for the lockers, I look up and see the man himself watching me from the window of his office. He's holding a cell phone to his ear and his mouth is moving, but it's clear his attention is solely fixed on me.

I wonder why the hell he's doing this.

7

SLOANE

"No, that's fine. I don't mind. I was…I was kind of hoping to go out for a drink with Oliver tonight anyway." I don't lie to Zeth. I know he won't like me going out with Oliver, but he's not my keeper. He's never tried to be. And besides, it sounds like he's got his hands full with this new kid at the gym. He called to tell me he was going to be home late, so he really can't say anything at all about me heading out after work.

And so he doesn't. Not a word.

"Zeth? Are you plotting ways to kill my friend?"

"No. Just thinking."

"You're not angry?"

"Should I be? Is he gonna try and lay his hands on you?"

"No."

"Then Oliver Massey is of little concern to me, Sloane." I can hear the wicked smile in the tone of his voice. "I mean, why the hell would I need to worry about him when you have me, anyway?"

He's an arrogant bastard sometimes, but he makes me laugh. He also has a really good point. There isn't a man alive on this planet that can come close to being anywhere near as sexy, thrilling, scary, alluring, or terrifying as him, all in one go. "Good to know your ego's fighting fit this evening," I laugh.

"Every part of me is fighting fit, Sloane. Always."

"Oh, god, I'm going before your modesty overwhelms me and I fall to my knees in worship."

"I like when you're on your knees, worshipping me. Or worshipping a certain part of my body, anyway."

Just hearing him talk about me going down on him makes my body tremble a little. I thought my inexperience in that field would mean I would be terrible at it, but turns out, despite how Zeth has command over me at every other single moment we're in bed together, I have total power over him when I use my mouth.

As I hang up the call, being wrapped up in him, feeling his hands over me, his mouth on me, my mouth on him… it's all I can think about.

I don't think I'll ever get enough.

My thoughts of Zeth are rudely interrupted three minutes later by my pager—911. An emergency. Great. And there was me thinking I was going to get out of the hospital at a reasonable hour tonight.

∼

A drunk driver smashes through the central reservation of the freeway, hits a school bus carrying twenty-three teenagers home from a trip to McCaw Hall, where they were seeing Swan Lake. Five teenagers are dead. Thirteen are injured. The drunk driver went head first through the windscreen of his Tacoma, and the EMTs have reported visible brain matter on the scene.

Who do you help first?

Oliver is shouting something over the bedlam taking place in the emergency room. I can barely hear him, but I've gotten pretty damn good at reading lips since I started this gig. He has a kid with internal bleeding who needs an urgent CT scan. He's taking her upstairs right now. Meanwhile, I'm stuck with the guy on the gurney who, I'm pretty sure, would go up in smoke if he were anywhere near an open flame. Flammable skin, flammable clothing, flammable breath, for crying out loud. By the smell of it, his pungent odor is because he's been bathing in Jim Beam. And drinking his bath water while he was at it.

I hear Oliver this time. "You gonna be okay down here?" he yells.

I give him a short, curt nod, which is all he needs before he vanishes through the swinging doors toward the elevator with his patient. Somewhere on the ER floor, a girl starts screaming at the top of her lungs. She's not in pain. I know what agonized screams sound like all too well. No, she's grieving. Make that six dead from the school bus.

As doctors, we're not allowed to differentiate between our patients while we're helping them. They could be serial killers, mass murderers, rapists, drug dealers…we're not allowed to treat them any differently than we would if we were treating any other civilian. That's not to say staying calm is easy, though. And it sure as hell isn't easy to refrain from cursing them as you assess the damage to their bodies.

"Fucking asshole," I growl, unwinding the temporary bandaging the paramedics have put around the guy's head. He moans something, maybe in pain, and I nearly drop the shard of his skull that falls out of the packing material. Holy shit. They weren't wrong about the brain matter. The guy has a two-inch wide hole in his head, and I'm holding the missing piece of his cranium in my hand, complete with scalp and hair.

A long time ago, I remember when the very sight would have turned me green and had me vomiting in the intern's bathroom. Now, the piece of this guy I'm holding in my hand is nothing more than a broken part of a machine that I have to fix.

Hours later—hours, and hours and *hours*—I emerge from the operating room, feeling rather pleased with myself. Not only did I manage to fix the hole in the driver's head, but I also had to think fast and mend his internal bleeding. Jerk didn't deserve the time we spent on him, perhaps, but hey. At the end of the day, it's not my job to judge people. It's my job to make sure they're alive so someone else can in a court of law.

When I hit the locker room, Massey is waiting

for me with a grin on his face. "How's your brother?" I ask.

"He's stable and conscious. Hence the shit-eating grin I'm wearing right now. Time to celebrate."

Relief floods me when I hear Oliver's news about his brother. I've been thinking about him constantly, wondering if we did enough to guarantee his recovery. "That's amazing, Ol. Thank fuck for that, huh? But as for celebrating… once again, we're finishing work after the bars have closed. Looks like we're gonna need another rain check on that drink."

"Nuh-uh. You're not getting out of it that easy, Romera."

"Unless you're planning on drinking the swabbing alcohol, which I highly do *not* recommend, then I'm afraid we have no other choice." Truth be told, I'm exhausted now. Bed is sounding like an amazing option.

Oliver grins at me some more, sliding his hand into his backpack and pulling out a bottle of red wine. "I have another one of these," he says. "Just in case. You and me, we're going up to the roof and we're not coming down until this is empty."

I'm weary right down to my very bones, but I can tell just from looking at him that Oliver is wired. He's clearly right: I'm not getting out of it that easily.

"All right, fine. But I have to make sure I'm home before the sun comes up, okay?"

"Why? Your boyfriend have you on curfew now?" Oliver says this jestingly, but there's a bite to his voice.

"Of course not. I'm just being considerate." And, of course, if Zeth wakes up and I'm not home in bed beside him, he's going to assume I was kidnapped by some of his old friends and I'm in very grave danger. That would be a very bad turn of events. He would tear this city apart and then set it on fire looking for me.

Oliver just shrugs his shoulders. "Whatever. Let's go." Up on the roof, memories hit me one after the other—all the times my father brought me up here with Alexis to watch the snow fall. I've been up here many times since, but every single time, this happens. My dad, Alexis and I, all holding hands, necks craning back, gentle snowflakes falling onto our faces, sticking to our eyelashes. There's no snow falling tonight, though. It's too warm. The skies are overcast, but the clouds are heavy with rain instead. Shame we can't see the stars. "Better get this show on the road, Romera," Oliver laughs. "Looks like we might get drenched if we take too long."

"So basically, you want to get drunk as fast as possible? Am I understanding you clearly? Just so we're on the same page."

Walking over to the very edge of the roof, Oliver sits himself down, legs dangling over the edge into the void. He removes one of the bottles from his bag and holds it out to me. "You know me so well."

"Yeah, well, you're a very smart man. Speaking of which, kudos to you for remembering to get twist-off caps this time." The last time I drank wine with Olly, we ended up stealing a butter knife from the canteen and shoving the cork down into the bottle. Suffice it to say, we both ended up covered in red wine, and our glasses were mostly filled with fragments of cork.

"I learned my lesson, obviously." Oliver takes out the other bottle of wine from his bag, and I realize the one he just handed to me is exactly that: mine. Neither of us have glasses, so we pop open the bottles, chink them together and drink straight from the bottle.

"We're so classy," I laugh.

"We're under a lot of pressure. If it means that we have to drink like hobos in order to unwind, then so be it, right?"

"Right."

I've nearly finished my bottle, feeling very sideways and most definitely drunk, when the sky opens up. The force of the raindrops as they hit the hospital roof is awe-inspiring. The sound of it roars in my ears as Oliver slumps to lie on his back, arms stretched out wide, his bottle of Malbec still gripped tightly in his right hand. "Wooohooo!" he hollers. "We're alive, Dr. Romera. We are fucking *alive*." Grabbing hold of me, he pulls me down so that I'm lying beside him in the torrential downpour, his words resonating inside my head.

I am alive. I am alive. After everything that happened, I somehow made it through to the other side. Even more miraculously, so did Zeth. I have a lot to be grateful for. I'm thick with emotion and soaked to the bone when the rain stops. Tiredness seems to hit Oliver; one second he's telling me about a procedure he perfected earlier when he was working on one of the school bus girls, and then the next he's scrambling to his feet on unsteady legs, telling me he has to go home. Immediately.

"You gonna throw up, mister?"

"Hell, no! When have you ever seen Oliver Massey throw up from alcohol?"

Yeah, that's actually true. I never have seen him sick from drinking too much. Never even seen him drunk at all, for that matter. He's most certainly a little worse for wear now, though. The giveaway is that he's referring to himself in the third person. I smile up at him, shivering. "Then why are you suddenly so desperate to leave? You gave me so much shit for never hanging out with you and then the next thing I know you're bolting."

He takes in a deep breath and blows it out quickly, scrubbing his hands through his wet hair. "I have to go because I'm about to try and kiss you. And your boyfriend knows people who can have me killed. Right?"

Oh. Oh, no. I can feel my smile turning sad. "Ah, yeah…. If you did that, Zeth wouldn't be hiring someone else to kill you. I'm pretty sure he'd do it himself."

"*Great.*"

"I'm not being a bitch, Ol. It's just what would happen."

"I know. I just…" Oliver scrunches up his face, closing his eyes. "Fuck it. Do you *want* me to kiss you?" Before I can react, before I can shake my head and tell him no, Oliver saves me. "Oh shit. Don't even answer that. I don't know what's wrong with me. I thought nothing would change. I thought I could ignore it. I thought hanging out would be the same. It's not. I just…I gotta go." He picks up his jacket and flings it over his shoulder. "You wanna come down with me now?"

I can tell he doesn't want me to. I can tell he just wants to run away. "No, that's okay. I'm just gonna sit here and—" *Freeze to death? Shiver so violently that my teeth grind into dust? Anything but have to bid you an awkward farewell downstairs in the parking lot.* I love Oliver to death, but it's pretty clear to me that things can never be as they once were between us. There's no going back. That makes me suddenly, overwhelmingly very sad.

"Okay, Romera. Well make sure you get home safe, okay? Make sure you catch a cab."

"I will. Good night." I tuck my chin into the crook of my arms, hugging myself as I wait for him to go. I'm ridiculously cold by the time I head back inside myself.

My clothes make wet slapping sounds as I kick out of them and toss them on the locker room floor.

8

SLOANE

My head is pounding when I crack my eyes open. Too bright. Too damn cold. The room pitches a little as I pull the covers up around my shoulders. "There she is," a voice says softly beside me. *Zeth*. His hands find me underneath the blankets, moving firmly over my body as he takes hold of me and pulls me close to him.

"Jesus, girl, you're burning up. You feeling okay?" he rumbles into my neck. A violent shiver rocks through me as his mouth moves languidly over my skin. The sensation is wonderful, but the shiver isn't because I feel good. It's because I'm feeling bad. Really, *really* bad.

"Oh, god. Oh, *no*."

"What is it?" Zeth bites at my ear lobe, his arms tightening around me.

"I think… I was out in the rain last night. I think I've caught a chill or something." Sure enough, when I breathe in through my nose, I'm all congested and stuffy. Damn it!

"I know what'll make you feel better." Zeth turns me slowly onto my back and climbs over me, his face hovering a couple of inches above my own. He looks deliciously tousled from sleep; his hair is much longer than I've ever seen it. He could style it now if he wanted to, yet at this particular moment it's sticking out in every which direction, begging me to tease it between my fingers. I do so, groaning at the ache in my joints. Movement is not my friend.

"Oh, boy. It must be bad. The great Dr Romera is moaning like the world is coming to an end." His mouth moves to the hollow of my neck, where he grazes his teeth against my skin. I'm so torn between pulling the cover tight against me and clamping my eyes closed until the awful spinning in my head passes, or pulling the sexy guy on top of me closer and letting him have his way with me.

Thing is, I'm feeling very delicate right now. "I don't think I can handle sex with you right now," I moan. "Your usual ministrations might just break me." I can't even believe I'm saying this. I never thought I'd be turning Zeth Mayfair down.

He kisses my chin, then the apple of each of my cheeks in turn. "Sloane?" He continues to kiss me, gently lowering himself onto me, so I can feel just how badly he wants me. His cock is hard, pressing gently against my stomach, making me even more conflicted. "*Sloane?*"

"Mmm?" I hiss when he rubs his cheek against mine, his stubble scratching at my skin in the most delicious way. "You shouldn't kiss me," I whisper. "I don't want you to get si—"

He cuts me off, pressing his lips firmly against mine. I think he may not have been paying attention to what I'm saying at first, but then I realize he's done it on purpose. His tongue teases the crease of my lips until I eventually give in and open my mouth to him. The kiss is deep and sweet and wonderful. He tastes so incredible, even first thing in the morning before brushing his teeth. Not too long ago, I couldn't have imagined this. He waited to kiss me for so long. Weeks and weeks and weeks. It was pure torture. Now, it seems like he doesn't want to stop.

Eventually, he has to.

"You're crazy," I whisper.

"If being sick means I still get to kiss you and be inside you, then bring it on. And also," he says, gently rocking his hips against mine, "who said anything about my usual ministrations?"

"What, no black bag?"

"Not this morning," he whispers, grinding himself against me. "Open your eyes."

I do. The tone of his voice is intense, full of some hidden message I'm not sure I understand. When I look into his eyes, I see what's there, though—he loves me. He fucking loves me, and I've been grumbling, absorbed with how terrible I feel. My worsening condition doesn't seem that important anymore. I'm intrigued by what he has in store for me. "Oh really?"

"Mmmm." His lips vibrate against my skin as he hums. "You want to try something different?"

"How different?" I peer up at him, wondering at the fierce look on his face.

"Well…" He almost looks like he's about to smile. No matter how crappy I'm feeling, my heart swells in my chest at the sight of his lips lifting at either side of his mouth. It's the most amazing thing. It's addicting. He dips his head and lightly rubs his nose against the bridge of my own. "How about you let me show you?"

"Okay." I whisper the word, half expecting to be caught up in a whirlwind of movement and tension and Zeth less than a second later, but that's not what happens. Instead, Zeth lets his weight down on top of me so he can take my face in his hands. He kisses me, deep and intense, his mouth working against mine in a slow, passionate rhythm that makes my bones feel like lead weights inside my body, making me heavy. Drunk. Dizzy. The way I feel could be attributed to the fact that I'm coming down with something, but then again it really doesn't feel that way. It's that desperate, adoring, all- powerful, all-consuming fire that I've never experienced myself but I've read about. This is what being in love is.

This is what falling even more deeply in love is, with each and every passing second. Cities could burn and the world could be ending, crashing down around my ears, and I wouldn't trade this feeling or this man to save a single soul. I just wouldn't be able to.

His hands move over my body slowly, curiously,

like he's never touched me before. We've had sex so many times now, but it's never been mechanical or rote. Every single inch of my skin has been explored and marked, claimed as his own, and yet when he touches me now it's as though he's still in wonder of me. Still completely obsessed with the texture and softness of my curves.

"You're so fucking beautiful, Sloane," he whispers into my hair. I feel like I've been drugged. When he slides his hands down over me and in between my legs, my breathing has quickened, right alongside my heart rate. He makes me feel incredible. "Close your eyes," he whispers. His voice is thick with the fire that's burning up within his own body. I don't really want to close my eyes—watching him like this is the most amazing thing I've ever experienced—but then again, falling into myself, letting him own me, sinking into the pleasure of his naked body against mine is amazing in its own right.

His fingers work over my clit, teasing me, driving me crazy. I'm completely absorbed in the sensation, wanting to beg him, plead with him for more, but there's no rushing this man. He'll give me what he wants to give me and when. And besides, the pure torture of it is delicious.

Zeth gathers my right wrist in his free hand, and

then the left, lifting both up over my head. He slides off me to one side so he doesn't crush me, and then he pushes my legs apart, opening me to him. I don't fight against him. My legs fall open, and then he has access to all of me. He makes good use of that access, his fingers tracing up and down over my pussy, setting me on fire as he teases my clit, gently dipping his index finger inside me, and then moving further down to lightly stroke an area of my body I never thought I'd allow anyone to touch. *Ever*.

With him, there are no taboos, though. No area of me off limits. No part of me I'll ever deny to him. Especially when he makes me feel this good.

"You gonna come for me, angry girl?" he says into my ear. He's breathless; I can feel his heart thumping in his chest, where his skin is pressed up against me.

"Yes."

"You want to come hard?"

"Yes."

"I want to feel you all over my fingers, okay? I want to know exactly when you're about to explode."

"Oh my god. Fuck, oh my god." But *he* is my god. He's the sun and I'm the earth, orbiting him always, unable to escape his gravity. Unwilling to try.

"Come for me, Sloane. Come on. Do it."

I've never been able to hold back with him. I have this overwhelming need to do what he wants me to, despite how much I fought against that idea when we first met. And right now, he wants me to come. He makes this pretty damn easy for me when he slides his fingers all the way inside, twisting them toward him and making a beckoning motion that tips me right over the edge.

I'm incapable of making a sound as my body locks up, gripped by the sheer force of the orgasm that hits me. It feels like I'm slamming into a brick wall.

Zeth growls deep in his throat as I writhe against him; he holds onto my wrists, stopping me from reaching out to touch him. I want to so badly, but I can tell by the firm grip of his hand that he doesn't want me to.

"Fuck, your body looks incredible like that. All stretched out and long, with your arms over your head," he says, his voice deep and filled with promises. I'm still coming, synapses snapping and firing blindly in my head as he stoops to take one of my nipples in his mouth. He licks and sucks at me, squeezing my nipple in-between his teeth as I squirm, trying to catch my breath.

"Are you ready for me, angry girl? Do you want me inside you? Is that what you want?"

I nod my head, burying my face in his shoulder as he continues to work his fingers inside me. Zeth doesn't wait for me to regain my voice; he accepts my nodding as all the permission he needs. He's inside me a second later, strong, hard body between my legs, his hands pulling my thighs up and around his waist. This is normally where he would fuck me until I can't see straight. I'm expecting it, holding my breath, waiting for it, and yet it doesn't happen. Opening my eyes, my heart still charging beneath my ribcage, I find Zeth staring down at me with a look akin to complete awe on his face. He just shakes his head, half smiling as he begins to move inside me.

It's torturous. Slow. Purposeful and intense. I've never experienced anything like it. And the whole time, Zeth doesn't look away. He holds me in his gaze as he fills me, carefully bringing me back to the point of frenzy. My body is crying out for him to sink himself deeper, harder, faster inside me, but my head knows that's not what this moment is right now. I'm too scared to even admit what this moment is.

Zeth's hands stroke my body as we move together, and it's almost as if I can feel it happening.

This is more than just our bodies connecting. This is something else entirely.

When we come, we come together, and it's silent. Zeth wraps his arms around me and I cling to him, and it feels like he's absorbed me into him. I have the most insane, obscene urge to cry. Why the fuck do I want to cry? I can't let it happen. If I do, he'll think I'm one of those crazy bitches who start sobbing after sex in the movies, and that is the very last thing I want. Instead, I press my face into the skin of his chest, eyes closed, trying to remember what my life looked like before he was in it. All I can remember is darkness.

Zeth slowly rolls us over, still inside me, so that he's lying on his back and I'm lying on top of him. There isn't a second where he removes his arms from around me. He holds on tight, like he's afraid I'm about to vanish into thin air. I can hardly breathe around the burning in my throat as his huge hands, used for so many years for violence, for inflicting pain, carefully stroke my hair.

9

ZETH

Something is really fucking wrong with me. When I left the house this morning, Sloane was sniffing and coughing, and all I wanted to do was stay home and take care of her. I had no idea how to do that, though, so I left instead. Feeling fucking useless is not my wheelhouse. My wheelhouse is smashing shit up and making people feel decidedly *worse* than before they met me. I don't have the first clue how to make someone feel *better*.

And the sex?

I don't even want to think about the sex. It was fucking insane in the very best way. Six months ago I'd have laughed hysterically at the very prospect of being intimate like that with someone. Sex has always been an outlet for some of my more exotic proclivities; it sure as shit has *never* been an outlet for affection. Or a display of love.

As I drive toward the gym, I bite the bullet. I let the guy from before, the guy I was for years, have free rein. *What the* fuck *are you doing, asshole? She's just some piece of ass. She's going to ruin you if you let her. Women come and go. They don't sleep in your bed. They don't make you coffee in the morning. And you don't fucking make love to them! You fuck. You fight. You flee. That's always been the rule, man. What the hell is wrong with you?*

What would Charlie think?

My stomach feels like it's full of ice-cold water at that last thought. For years, what Charlie thought or wanted or cared about was all that concerned me. The fucker tried to kill me repeatedly. He stole into my room every night for years, playing his fucked-up mind games with me, and yet still some desire to please him is ingrained deep within my bones. The guy's dead and even now I can't escape him. How fucked up is that?

I'm almost at the gym when my cell starts ringing. Assuming it's Michael, I almost answer it without thinking. The out-of-state number on the display catches my eye, though. I stare at the screen for a moment, debating whether to answer. On the sixth ring, I make up my mind. This had better be fucking good.

I pick up, and I don't say a motherfucking word.

I'm met with silence, and then, "What's up, asshole? Roberto Barbieri asked us to call you."

Barbieri? What the fuck? The name has instant alarm bells ringing in my head. Barbieri and Charlie used to have some dealings back in the day. The Italians are based out of New York, but they're always looking to move in on new territory. I suppose I shouldn't be surprised that I'm hearing from them now. Seattle has been a largely unclaimed territory for months. In fact, this probably should have happened much sooner.

"Roberto Barbieri shouldn't even have this number," I growl into the phone. There are sounds of a scuffle on the other end of the line, and then another voice speaks. These are the brothers, Theo and Sal. Barbieri's sons. Their reputations precede them, just like mine does. And from the calm tone and the fierce intelligence I can hear in this guy's voice, I'm talking to the older brother right now—Theo.

"Mr. Mayfair, we met back in Seattle a couple of months ago. I believe we had a common enemy. The Monterellis? You took care of one brother. We took care of the other."

Huh. I'd had my suspicions about that. I did end Frankie Monterelli, yes. He was the last person I killed, and the fucker had been going for his gun. When his younger brother, Archie Monterelli, was killed at St. Peter's Hospital, things really started to get complicated for me. "I remember," I say. "The cops pinned me for that one, too. Made life very difficult for me and my girl."

"We're sorry about that. The method of execution's usually enough to tip the cops off over here in New York." The method of execution being a Columbian Necktie. I remember Sloane telling me the blood had hit the damn ceiling. Not my style at all.

"Seattle cops don't know shit about Roberto Barbieri. And they don't care, either. You guys made a mess."

"Irrespective of what happened, Roberto wants to hire you. He's offering big money for you to fly out to New York."

"I don't work for other people, *Theo.*" I throw in the name just to let him know I'm aware of exactly who he is. I can almost feel the fucker squirming on the other end of the line.

"You'd be a contractor. My father would give you free rein to handle the job however you pleased. You'd be here for a couple of days, do the work and then you'd be flying home again. Simple."

Well that's fucking strange. I thought for sure this would be about claiming the city that Charlie Holsan left behind. And now it looks like Barbieri wants me to do a job for him in New York? That's bullshit. He has plenty of morons on hand to pull the trigger of a gun. His sons, for instance. No, this *is* about Seattle. The bastard's just being sneaky about it.

"The kind of jobs your father hires men like me for are never simple. I'm west coast these days, Theo. And I don't kill people for money anymore. Tell your father thanks but no thanks. Don't call this number again." I hang up before he has chance to say anything else. There isn't a single thing he could say to me to change my damn mind. I have a very clear vision of how I want my life to be in the future, and getting caught up in this shit does not feature whatsoever.

No, you're all about the white picket fence now, huh, motherfucker?

I've forgotten to shove the old me back into the vault. He thinks all of this is highly fucking entertaining. I brush the thought aside, determined not to let my jacked-up past dictate how I think and feel now. I won't let what's gone before ruin what could be. If I did, that would make for a really shitty life indeed. I wonder what Pippa, Sloane's sometimes best friend and my sometimes therapist would make of me torturing myself like this. She hates me, but she'd probably try and talk me down. Try and make me cut myself some slack. Fuck. I'm probably due an appointment with the woman, but damned if I wouldn't rather shove burning-hot pokers into my eyes right now.

Michael's waiting for me outside the gym when I pull up and park the Camaro. His grim expression matches my own. I take one look at him and I know something is wrong.

I sigh, jamming my hands in my pockets, letting my chin drop to my chest. "What? What the fuck is it now?"

Michael's mouth pulls into a flat line; I do *not* like the concerned look in his eyes. "Lowell," he says. "Detective Lowell's back in town. And she's got a fucking *army* of DEA agents with her."

10

SLOANE

One of the benefits of being a doctor is that you can get your friends to write you a prescription whenever you need one without too much hassle. Pippa, my best friend, gave me a script for Valium once when I really needed it, and she didn't ask a single question. Oliver Massey doesn't ask me any questions either, as he writes me out a script for antibiotics. He doesn't need to. I have my own pad out and I'm writing him the same script. We're both sick as dogs.

"Seemed like such a good idea at the time, huh?" he groans. So far he's pretended that he didn't say anything to make our lives really awkward the other night, even though he really did. "My mom used to tell me sitting out in the rain would give me hypothermia. I never believed her."

"Stop being so melodramatic. You've seen hypothermia. This is *not* hypothermia. This is the *flu*, and it really sucks, but these," I wave the two pieces of paper bearing our signatures in the air, "are going to fix us right up. You ready?"

He nods gravely. We head down to the pharmacy and collect our medication, grumbling the entire way. I cough and sneeze, while he holds his palm against the side of his head and takes very deep breaths, complaining about the room spinning. I feel like I already went through that stage this morning. He's still got the congestion and the rattling lungs to look forward to.

"What in god's name is wrong with you two?" The voice—it takes a while to spin around and see who's standing behind us—belongs to Rebecca Allison, the Chief of Medicine at St Peter's Hospital.

"Oh, it's nothing. We're fine. We're good to go," Oliver says quickly. He only grimaces a little as he stands up straight.

Chief Allison pulls a face—her *don't-try-and-pull-*

that-shit-with-me face. She darts forward and holds the back of her hand against Oliver's forehead. There might have been a time when she would have checked me first, but the woman still hasn't forgiven me for the crazy stuff that went down here recently. Crazy stuff that I was heavily involved in, and nearly got people killed.

She prods Oliver in the chest, apparently not liking what she finds when she tests his temperature. "*You* are already on my shit list for that stunt you pulled treating your own brother. And now you're both recklessly endangering the entire medical staff by being here right now. What's wrong with you?" she hisses.

"It's really noth—"

"I don't want to hear it, Romera. Go home. Go to bed. Hell, I don't care where either of you go so long as you don't come back until you're fit and healthy. Get the hell out of my hospital. *Now!*"

11

MASON

I'm covered in shit and grease and I'm sweating like I've just run ten miles when she comes into the shop. Short, cropped blonde hair that barely grazes her jawline, and stellar blue eyes that are exactly cornflower blue. I feel fucking ridiculous that I even know what color cornflower blue is. Can't say I've ever even thought about that color, but as soon as I look up and see her standing there, it's the first damn thing that pops into my head. She's wearing skinny jeans and a huge parka with fur trim around the hood, hands shoved into her pockets, smoke pluming on her breath. Beautiful. Seriously, the most beautiful thing I've ever seen in my entire life. A smile pulls at her mouth when those blue eyes see me watching her as she talks to Mac, and I suddenly have an overwhelming urge to bury my head in the car engine I'm working on and not look up again until she's gone. No such luck, though.

"Mason, get your ass over here," Mac calls. I shoot the bastard an evil glare as I wipe my hands on an oily rag, doing as I'm told. He doesn't even notice that I'm drilling holes into his head as I make my way over to them. "Mason, this young lady has a problem with her car. She's running late to her… wait, what did you say you were studying again?"

The blonde with the huge coat and the cold-reddened cheeks smiles, flashing perfectly straight, perfectly white teeth. Up this close, she looks like a little porcelain doll. Or a pixie. Yeah, that's more appropriate. She looks like something out of one of the books I read to Millie before she goes to bed. There's something ethereal about her.

"I'm doing social studies," the girl says. "I'm in my final year at Seattle University." Her voice is high and clear, confident, yet with a hint of nerves. I glance at her out of the corner of my eye—direct eye contact seems like a horrific idea—and I can see she's smiling at me.

"Yeah, that's right. Social studies, whatever that is," Mac says gruffly. "She's gonna leave her car with me while you run her over to her class."

"What? I thought you wanted the Firebird finished by midday?" I don't want to drive this beautiful, frightening creature the whole way across the city. Eye contact would be completely unavoidable. As would small talk, and I'm no fucking good at small talk.

Mac just raises his eyebrows at me. "Faster you get going, faster you get back, right?" He tosses the keys to the shop's run around at me; Mac bought a very sensible, reliable Volvo for this very purpose. It's an extra service people travel specifically to the shop for, since they know they can get a ride while their own cars are being worked on. Normally I'd be jumping at the chance to get the hell out of here for an hour, but for some reason my heart feels like a clenched fist rising up in my throat.

"Come on. I'll let you choose the radio station," the girl says, heading toward the Volvo.

As soon as she's out of earshot, Mac thumps me

really fucking hard on the arm and grins. "You can thank me later, kid."

"Fucking thank you with my fist, asshole," I grumble under my breath. The girl tosses her bag onto the backseat and then gets in the passenger side, and I climb into the driver's side, dreading the next thirty minutes.

As I pull out of the shop, I see Zeth on the other side of the street, standing outside the gym with that friend of his. They both look seriously pissed, lost in conversation as I pull out and drive by with the midget blonde sitting beside me. If they see me, they don't acknowledge me. A good thing right now, I think; I wouldn't want those stern expressions directed toward me. No way, no how.

"So you're a mechanic, huh?"

I grip the steering wheel with both hands. Millie would be rolling her eyes at me right now. For a five year-old, the kid sure does have attitude. "Yeah. Apparently."

The girl beside me nods. "*Apparently.*" She pulls a face, like she's pretending to be mulling this over. She turns her head toward me and places her cheek against the headrest, her attention solely fixated on me. "I'm Kaya." I steal another sideways glance at her, and there it is: eye contact. Damn. She blinks at me in a rather owlish fashion. "Aren't you going to tell me your name?"

"You already know my name. Mac told you."

"But it's nice to have a proper introduction, right?" She's still looking at me. Still not looking away. Fuck.

"Mason." My name comes out clipped, like I resent parting with it. I can see the girl—Kaya—nodding her head thoughtfully out of the corner of my eye.

"You're not very comfortable right now, are you?"

"Not particularly."

"And why is that?"

I draw in a deep breath through my nose, not sure how to respond. "I don't know. I'm just not."

"Just not? Bit of a lame answer, don't you think?"

"I just—"

"You just think I'm pretty and you don't know how to talk to me?"

"*What?*" This girl has absolutely no filter. And apparently no sense of modesty, either.

"You think I'm pretty. It's okay, I think you're pretty too."

"I am *not* pretty."

"Yes, you are. In a way." She laughs, fog still on

her breath inside the car. Weird, because I feel like I'm burning up. I lean over and hit the heating anyway.

"Guys aren't pretty. They're hot or handsome or whatever," I say.

"You'd prefer me to tell you that I think you're hot?"

"I don't care what you call me."

"Sure you do." That laughter again. Kaya pivots in her seat, turning her whole body to face me now. "Aren't you really tired of these veiled conversations you have with people, day in, day out? Wouldn't it just be so much more *interesting* if you said what you were thinking?"

"Is that how you are? All the time?"

"Mmm-hmm." I hear a snapping sound. She's produced some red vines from somewhere and is ripping pieces off with her teeth. Grinning, she breaks some off with her fingers this time and offers it out to me. She is perhaps the strangest person I have ever met. I take the red vine and bite down on it, feeling completely out of my depth. This is not something I enjoy doing. Girls are an enigma to me at the best of times. Don't get me wrong. I'm not a virgin by any stretch of the imagination. But interacting with women has always seemed like some complex puzzle I haven't had time to figure out. Not with Millie to look after.

"Life's just very short, Mason. I don't like to waste time. By the end, when I die, I want to look back and know that I climbed mountains and jumped out of planes with the time other people wasted talking about the goddamn weather."

"I suppose that's something to aspire to."

"Isn't it, though?" Kaya leans across the console between us and my head is suddenly full of the sweet scent of flowers and something else, like jasmine. She's so damn close. Her face is just inches away from mine.

"What the hell are you doing?"

"Looking at you," she whispers. "Looking at your eyes."

"Why?" She's so perplexing. I have absolutely no idea why she would need to be looking at my eyes. Especially this frickin' close.

"I'm into Kinesiology. You can tell a lot about a person from their eyes."

"Like they're the windows to the soul?" My voice drips with derision. I feel like a dick even as I'm saying it, but I can't stop myself. Mom used to be into that hippy dippy shit. All I saw when I looked in her eyes was broken blood vessels and the same haunted desperation all junkies wear.

Kaya shakes her head, smiling softly, like she was expecting better of me. "Not quite. It's more to do with physical illness. Tension and stress in your body. That kind of thing."

"So what about me? Am I physically ill?"

I can see her shaking her head slowly again. "Don't think so. Hard to tell." I expect her to tell me she needs to get a better look—I'm already trying to come up with an excuse as to why I'm not going to let her gaze deeply into my eyes—but she doesn't. We sit in silence for a moment, the city passing us by out the window, Seattle University getting closer and closer. I'm so fucking desperate to get her there as quickly as possible that I barely pay attention to where I'm going. Our journey takes us past Mil's school; the kids are out at recess and the sound of children screaming and laughing sets me on edge. My sister's always so fucking quiet. Her teachers tell me she doesn't really interact all that much. When I asked her about it, she sat there and stared at the floor for what felt like a fucking age, and then she whispered that they made fun of her. Made fun of her because she had a seizure one time and wet herself and now they all avoided her like the plague. Like the poor kid is some kind of leper or something. Such fucking bullshit.

"What are you thinking about right now?"

Kaya speaks softly but her words snap me out of the black tunnel I was falling head first into.

"Huh?"

"What are you thinking about? You look like you're trying to rip the steering wheel right out of the dashboard."

Sure enough, my knuckles are white, locked around the steering wheel, my fingers digging into my own palms as I grip on tightly. It takes effort to relax my hands. "Nothing." I clear my throat. "Just trying to concentrate." Kaya makes an amused sound, shifting in her seat. As she swivels around to face forward, it feels like some sort of wall has gone up between us. "What? Is concentrating not allowed?"

"Sure it is."

"Then what?"

"I just thought you weren't going to be one of *those* people."

"One of what kind of people?"

"The bullshit kind." She pulls out more red vines from the pocket of her massive jacket. This time she doesn't offer me any. "The small talk kind. The kind who tell small, pointless lies instead of just being honest."

"I don't even fucking know you. Why would I just start spilling my shit to you?" She doesn't say anything. The silence is the pointed kind—the kind designed to make you uncomfortable. "Jesus. Why do you even care?"

"Because you looked sad, Mason. And I've dealt with sad my whole life. It's a lonely place."

"You're digging into my shit because you think I'm *lonely*?"

"Yeah, maybe. Right now, I'm reassessing, though. There's a strong possibility that you're just an asshole."

"Yeah. Now you're getting the picture." My hands inadvertently tighten around the steering wheel again.

"What are you doing tonight?"

"*What?*"

"What are you doing tonight? I think you should take me out on a date."

I can't really believe what I'm hearing right now. This chick makes absolutely no sense whatsoever. "You're here in this car with me right now, right? You've been present for this conversation? What about the last twenty minutes has convinced you that a date in on the cards for us?"

"Don't you like me, Mason? If you drop me off at school right now and you never see me again, aren't you going to wonder about me? Next week, won't you be thinking, *man, I should have asked that kinda crazy girl out on a date?*"

"So you realize you're kinda crazy, then? It's not just me."

"You haven't answered the question."

I let out a deep sigh. She's exhausting. Maybe that's why I give in and do what she wants me to do. I tell the truth. "Fuck, fine. Yeah. I guess, maybe, for some stupid, *insane* reason, I might be wondering what would have happened if I asked you out on a date. But then I would experience a moment of clarity and realize that I probably dodged a bullet."

"Just do it, Mason."

"What?"

"Ask me out." Kaya snaps more of the red vine off with her front teeth.

"I can't take you out tonight," I tell her. "I have a thing."

"What kind of thing?"

I almost feel like laughing. She strikes me as the touchy feely type. No way is she going to like this. "I have a fight. I'm going to be beating the crap out of someone."

"Cool. At French's?"

I do my best not to look absolutely stunned. She knows about French's? There's a very select few people in this city that know about the underground fighting ring that sets up underneath La Maison Markets every Saturday night. She doesn't even sound *fazed* by what I've told her. "Yeah, that's right. You go?" It sounds like a ridiculous question, even as I'm asking it.

"My brother fights there every weekend." She sounds perfectly bored.

"Huh. What's his name?" Like I would know his damn name. Tonight is my first night fighting. I won't know a single person there, apart from my buddy, Ben, and he's in the higher ups. He won't be able to babysit my ass for me. I'm going to be flying solo.

"Jameson. His name is Jameson Rayne."

I feel my own damn breath catching in my throat. For a second there I feel like I'm choking. *"Jameson Rayne is your brother?"* Jameson was the youngest guy to take the pot at French's. He bet on himself and won upward of forty thousand dollars in one night, and all at the age of twenty-one. As far as I know, he's twenty-six now and he's still making bank betting on himself. No one ever wants to fight him. And why the hell would they? The guy's a savage bastard.

"Urgh, not you, too," Kaya says. She leans her forehead against the window, looking away from me. "Jameson Rayne, the world's most notorious fighter." She makes an agitated sound at the back of her throat. "Gets *really* fucking old."

"It's no fun having a badass for a brother?"

"Not when he's intensely protective and borderline crazy, no." Kaya absently holds out a whole red vine, still refusing to look at me. I accept it, kicking my own ass. I want her to look at me. I complained about those intense eyes studying me, picking me apart at the seams, trying to figure out what's inside, but now that they're focused elsewhere and it feels weird.

"Older brothers are meant to be protective over their younger sisters," I whisper.

"You say that like you have some sort of experience in the field."

"Maybe I do." I'm pulling into Seattle University, though, so I don't have to tell her about that. Thank fuck. Kaya jumps out of the car and grabs her bag from the back seat. When the door slams, I think that's it—she's just going to leave without saying another word to me— but then she's there by the driver's side window, tapping against the glass. I buzz the window down. "You never told me if I was right," she says.

"I'm sorry?"

"I said you thought I was pretty. Is that not the case?"

I just stare at her. She barely has to bend down to talk to me through the window, she's so small. Her eyes are bright, her cheeks still blushed red against the cold. She doesn't look like she belongs here. She looks like she's made out of something breakable. China, maybe. I have an overwhelming urge to protect her, to prevent her from ever breaking, but I can't. My hands are already too, too full.

"Of course I think you're pretty. I think you're fucking beautiful," I whisper. "But we're in different places. If things were different…"

"Oh, I know," she says, smiling. She doesn't seem pissed at the fact that I'm trying really fucking carefully to tell her I'm not interested. Even though I kind of am, which is the hardest part. "Don't worry. Whatever's meant to be always is, right?" She beams, pats her hand against the windshield, and then she's pulling the hood up on that gigantic Parka and walking away. I sit there and watch her as she runs up the steps into the building in front of me, feeling honorbound to make sure she gets inside safely. Once she vanishes, I do the sanest thing I can thing of: I speed out of the parking lot like the very devil himself is on my heels.

MASON

"Why do I have to sleep at Wanda's house?" Millie hugs her soft toy, Roo, to her little pigeon chest, the Winnie the Pooh character looking faded and more than a little worse for wear. My baby sister looks like she might cry. I suddenly feel really fucking sick.

"You don't have to if you don't want to, Mil. You want me to stay home here with you?"

She looks up at me with those big eyes of hers, shiny from the potential tears that might fall—she hasn't decided yet whether staying at Wanda's is a big enough deal to warrant tears—and blinks. "Where are you going?" she whispers.

"I'm going to do another job."

"But you went to work this morning." She rubs the pad of her index finger against my knee, staring at it, clad in my jeans, apparently absorbed in the feel of the material.

"I know, kiddo, but this is for extra. Extra money. So we can move and get a better place, right?" We've talked about this enough that Millie knows how important moving is for us. She gives me a very solemn nod, still not looking at me.

"Away from next door to Wanda and Brandy?" she asks.

"Well, yeah, Mil. Somewhere safe. Somewhere good, right?"

"Can Wanda and Brandy come?"

I have to bite my lip as I stare down at the wispy golden curls on the top of her tiny head. "I don't know, Mil. Maybe. I think Wanda likes living here, though. We can always come visit her and Brandy, can't we?" Of course Wanda doesn't like living in this shitty building with it's shitty pipes and drafty windows, but you end up telling lies like this to keep the peace. And to comfort, too. Besides, Millie is still going to come here after school while I'm still stuck at Mac's, so that part is true at least.

"So do you think I should stay?" I ask. I shouldn't really be giving her the choice, but she panics less if she thinks she's in control of what's happening and when. I mean, how fucked up is it that a little girl her age needs to feel like *she's* in control, because the world is too scary, and dangerous and frightening. It fucking stinks.

"No. No, you can go," she says quietly. She's silent for a moment and then her head snaps up, a broad smile spreading across her face. She holds her hands to her mouth, like she's afraid of even speaking the idea that has just occurred to her. "Um, if you get more money," she says carefully. "That means I can have a new princess bed."

This is stated like it's a foregone conclusion. Brandy, Wanda's daughter, got a fancy bed for Christmas—a mini four poster thing with pink frilly see-thru material that you can pull across to make a sort of den. Millie's never mentioned wanting one before, not once. She never asks for anything. But now, I can see from the look in her eyes that this is something she wants very badly. I feel like a piece of shit. A bed like that wouldn't cost a huge amount of money, but it's more than we have. More than I'm likely to bring home tonight from my very first fight.

"How about we see what happens, huh, kiddo?"

Millie nods, her head rising and falling in exaggerated movements. "Okay." She's all too happy to run next door with Roo underneath her arm, then, at the prospect of 'seeing what happens' with her getting a new princess bed. I'm all but forgotten. Wanda squeezes me tightly to her massive chest when she opens the door to us. I've nearly suffocated in that woman's cleavage more times than I can count.

"You be careful tonight, you hear me?" she scolds.

"As careful as I can be." I hold out the tiny backpack with the pink ponies firing rainbows out of their asses on the front of it—at least that's what it looks like—and Wanda takes it from me without a word. She knows what's inside: a clean pair of PJs, Millie's favorite blanket, and her expensive as fuck medication. Wanda knows the drill. She knows what she needs to give Mil if she has a seizure. The woman has never once complained about having to clean up after my sister if she has a fit. Not once.

She gives me another warm hug and then shoos me on my way, knowing exactly where I'm going, hating it, and yet still not telling me not to go. She knows this is the only way I'm going to change things for us.

It takes twenty minutes to drive across the city to La Maison French Markets. Of course, there are no markets taking place right now. The vendors have cleared out their tables and equipment, knowing that Saturday nights are fight nights. I park my shitty truck three streets away as I was instructed by Ben, and then I make my way over to the west entrance of the underground markets. There are already plenty of people slipping down the concrete staircase, doing their best to look inconspicuous and not pulling it off. There's hardly any point in trying to hide what goes on down here, really. The cops are already fully aware of what goes on, paid off to keep quiet and not cause a fuss or disrupt the evening's entertainment.

The stairwell smells like piss and stale sweat. Down one level, the large space is filled with bodies, all pushing and shoving against one another. The rush of voices bounces off the low ceiling, making the roaring rumble of shouted conversation and raucous laughter even louder. For a very brief moment, I consider turning around and getting the fuck out of here. It's all too much, and I have absolutely no business being here.

But then I remember Millie and that hopeful look in her eye when I kissed her goodnight, and my resolve solidifies. I'm not leaving. I'm staying, and I'm going to win my fucking match.

I find Ben at the side of the ring—an easy thing to do considering his red hair—handing over hundred-dollar bills to a morbidly obese guy in a sweat stained Cuban hat. My friend grins, slapping me on the shoulder when I arrive at his side. "There he is! Thought you'd pussied out, motherfucker. You're almost late. Hey, this is Carlos. You need to pay your cover to him, okay?"

The fat guy in the hat arches an eyebrow at me, his facial expression unchanging as he holds out his hand. I go to shake it, but he speaks before I can make contact. "That'll be five hundred, friend." He doesn't want to meet me. He wants my cash. And too fucking much of it.

"*Five hundred?*" I glance over at Ben, ready to pop him in the shoulder for lying to me. Ben's already holding up his hands, that look that he gets already forming on his face.

"Whoa, whoa, slow your roll, C. Mason's an initiate. It's one hundred for initiates, right?"

Carlos squints, running his tongue over his teeth. "Two fifty for initiates. Buy-in went up."

"When?"

"Just now," Carlos says, frowning up at the both of us from under drawn brows. He doesn't look like the kind of guy who particularly enjoys being questioned.

"That's bullshit," Ben argues.

"Maybe. He don't like it, he don't have to fight, though. Them's the breaks."

Ben sighs, shrugs, then casts me a questioning glance. *You got two fifty?* I shake my head. I was breaking a sweat over the potential of stumping up a hundred and losing it all. More than double that? I just don't have it. Ben nods, puts his hand into his pocket, and pays Carlos before I can stop him.

"What the fuck, man? No!" I hiss. "If I lose, I can't pay you back."

Carlos tuts as he puts the money into his back pocket and writes something down into a small, ratty book.

"S'okay, man. Just don't fucking lose," Ben advises, like it's the most obvius thing ever. "No pressure."

"Name?" Carlos clips out. "Hey, asshole. *What. Is. Your. Name?*"

"Mason Reeves."

That goes into his book. "Lose the shirt," he says. I take off my hoody and my shirt and stand there bare-chested as Carlos takes a fat red marker pen and scrawls something onto my left shoulder blade. "And you, dipshit." He prods his pen in Ben's direction.

Ben loses his t-shirt and Carlos draws a fat eighty-eight onto his shoulder, and then vanishes into the swell of the crowd, presumably to find more people to verbally abuse and draw on.

Ben whoops, slapping the top of my arm. "Turn around, man. Let me see what ranking he gave you. Oh shit!" he laughs. "Twelve? Damn!"

"Twelve? What the fuck does twelve mean?"

"Twelve percent chance of winning." Apparently this is the funniest shit ever, according to my so called best friend. Undoubtedly he only thinks it's so funny because Carlos gave him an eighty eight percent chance of winning, which means a shit ton more money from the house if he does. "Don't worry, man," he says, pulling me through the sea of bodies. "They always rank new guys low. He hasn't seen you fight yet. C'mon."

On the other side of the packed out market place, a ring has been set up and the first match of the night is already underway. The two guys in the ring are lean and quick, jabbing and striking at each other faster than lightning, barely grazing each other before darting out of reach. The crowd get bored of that pretty quickly. They want brutality. They want blood. They want the sound of bone cracking on bone. These violent things make the blood run hot in their veins.

Four minutes after we arrive, the two guys have been booed out of the ring, neither one of them having landed a proper punch, and two new fighters are climbing into the cage. Their fight is adrenalin fuelled from the moment the bell rings. One broken nose. A couple of potential broken ribs. One K.O. Two minutes and the whole thing is over. The people squeezing in around the cage are screaming at the tops of their lungs. I need a fight like that. I need something violent and bloody that will have them remembering my name until next weekend, where I'll have to prove myself all over again.

There are three more fights before I'm called up. At least two hundred people go silent as I shove my way past them and up through the opening into the cage. My heart is fucking hammering in my chest. This is such a bad fucking idea.

It gets worse when Carlos, motherfucker that he is, calls out the name of the guy I'm going to be fighting: Hail Mary Harris. Ben. Fucking *Ben*. It dawns on me all of a sudden—he's the other eighty eight percent to my twelve. How did I not immediately realize as soon as I found out my ranking. I mean, the maths were staring us right there in the face. Ben vaults up into the cage, shaking his head, his eyebrows drawn tight together.

"Fuck, Carlos. What the hell? It's his first night. I shouldn't be fighting initiates. And he shouldn't be fighting intermediaries, either. What gives?"

"We're short on fights tonight. Just the way it is, friend. You don't wanna fight, you can always concede." Carlos grins. He doesn't give a shit about the fact that he's making friends fight, and on top of that one friend who massively outranks the other.

Ben's still scowling when he faces me. The crowd can tell something's not right; they start chanting, pounding their feet against the floor, rattling the wire of the cage. *"Fight, fight, fight, fight, fight!"*

"You wanna back out, man?" Ben asks me.

"Hell no." The fighter who backs out sacrifices the money he paid in order to fight in the first place. I couldn't afford to lose the hundred I'd originally planned on spending, let alone the extra one fifty I now owe Ben. He nods.

"Okay. Well, I guess we're fighting then." He scratching his jaw, suddenly grinning like a mad man. "And I win either way, since I bought you in. Ironic, huh?"

"Yeah. Awesome." He looks way too pleased with himself right now.

"Are you ladies done gossiping or can we get this show on the road?" Carlos snipes.

Ben lifts his right fist, already gloved, and holds it out to me. "I'll go easy on you, I swear."

"Don't do me any favors, asshole." I touch my glove to his, the bell rings and that's it. No more time to talk. No more time to think. No more time to worry about what will happen if I lose this fight. My friend is circling me, a dark, predatory look in his eyes, and my head is *not* in the game. It gets there pretty quickly.

Ben comes for me, slamming his fist home straight between my guard, the same way Zeth did repeatedly the first time I fought him. My ears are ringing, my vision blurred when I step forward, trying to shake off the buzzing in my head. Ben's grinning, shrugging his shoulders, the light over out heads swinging crazily, casting evil shadows all over his face. I can see in his eyes that he thinks this is going to be ridiculously easy. And maybe it is. But I've never fought or even spared with Ben before, and Zeth did manage to give me a few invaluable pointers that cost me a number of nasty bruises. He doesn't know what I've got up my sleeve.

I let him land a hit on me again, this time to my side where Zee nearly broke some of my ribs. I wince, sucking oxygen into my lungs as best I can through the pain. Jesus fucking Christ.

I counter, landing a mean upper cut to Ben's jaw. The smile has vanished from his face when he cracks his neck, loosening out his shoulders.

"Ahhh, like that is it?" he says, laughing. Ben's a boxer. Has been for as long as I've known him. I'm willing to bet he hasn't spent nearly enough time practicing any other martial arts forms since he started fighting down here, knocking people out left, right and center.

We parry back and forth for thirty seconds, each landing blows where we can. I keep my fucking guard up, and I don't break eye contact with the guy. The crowd are baying for blood by the time I decide to test my theory. Ben comes in to land a left hook, but I'm ready for him. I duck, strike up, and then I slam into him, taking him down.

He makes a deep, surprised *uffff* sound as the air leaves his lungs. While he's trying to recover, I'm already moving, already planning my next move. Spinning him over, I twist his arm around into a lock and pull upward, looking for that sweetspot between what will mean absolute agony for him or a broken bone. I find that point when his body goes tense beneath me, rigid as a board.

"Motherfucker," he laughs. "Where the hell did that come from?"

Now's not the time to be cocky. I concentrate on what I'm doing, locking him down, making it impossible for him to move without extreme pain firing through his whole body. Maybe I'm concentrating too hard.

I'm ready for him when he tries to jerk me off him, using his hips to push backward. When he realizes I'm not going to let him off that easy, he rips his body around, growling against the discomfort of his arm nearly popping out of joint.

The next three seconds happen quickly. I'm on top of Ben in mount position, legs either side of him one second, and the next I'm on my back and Ben's hammering his fists into my face.

They call it ground and pound for a reason. I have to get out of this position. *Right. Fucking. Now.* Ben's too busy pummeling my face to guard any other area of his body. As his fists rain down, I somehow have the common sense to react. To move. To jab him as hard as I can. I am for his ribs, and pure determination takes over. I know I'm spraying blood everywhere from my mouth and my nose every time I gasp for breath, and I know Ben's doing his fair share of bleeding onto the canvas too, but neither one of us stop.

Eventually, Ben's winded enough that he pauses— just enough of an opening for me to get out from under him. It goes on like this for another three minutes, one of us bettering the other, the other taking a beating, and then the roles reversing over and over again. I'm so exhausted I can barely lift my arm anymore when the final bell rings.

The crowd starts hollering and screaming at the injustice of the fight being called to an end. Ben and I lay on our backs, chests heaving, blood all over our skin, in our hair, in our eyes, blood *everywhere*, and all I can focus on is the light swinging over my head, burning into my retinas, and the insanity of my heartbeat.

Carlos stands us up, clearly unhappy that Ben didn't just wipe the fucking floor with me. He holds Ben's arm in the air and the crowd cheers like crazy. Surprisingly, when he holds my arm in the air, the reaction is the same. A draw.

Well fuck me.

An hour passes where more people fight and me and Ben slump against the back wall, trying to get our shit together. Eventually Carlos comes and pays up the money he owes us, half each. Nine hundred dollars for me and nine hundred for Ben.

"Not bad for two black eyes and a mild concussion, huh?" Ben laughs. "Fuck, you punch like a heavy weight."

"Sorry, man," I sigh. Am I really sorry, though? Hell no. I hand over the one fifty he spotted me, feeling kind of amazing as I pocket what's left over. Seven hundred and fifty bucks. I wouldn't earn that working for Mac every day for two weeks. A couple of black eyes and a mild concussion were worth it all right.

13

ZETH

A pineapple sits on the kitchen counter. A *pineapple*. It's just not something you see everyday. It wasn't there when I went to bed last night, that's for sure. I'm all for eating fruit—you don't get a body like mine by shoving Twinkies down your throat twenty-four-seven—but this thing looks like it requires preparation. It's fucking spiky. I stand in the kitchen, staring at it for a while, contemplating how to proceed, and then I figure, *fuck it, I'll wing it* and go on a mission to find a knife.

Sloane got sent home from work yesterday, and is still asleep upstairs in our bed. *Our* bed. I never thought I'd be thinking those words. It gives me insane pleasure to run a playback of what took place in that bed yesterday in minute detail as I carve up the fruit for my girl's breakfast. There was a lot of spanking involved. And a tiny clamp that I hooked up to Sloane's clit, firing electrical charges into her sweet pussy that had her clawing at my skin and screaming out my name. I fucking love when she does that.

The memory of our heated sex is almost enough to put Agent Lowell and her damn skivvies out of my head. Michael's on the case. He's going to figure out what the hell she's doing back here, and then the two of us are going to figure out how we make her disappear again. As if he knows I'm thinking of his last owner, Ernie lifts his head from his paws where he's been sleeping by the back door and growls. Funny little bastard. I don't want to think about Lowell at all today, so I take a deep breath and exhale the stone-cold bitch right out of my head. Ernie sighs like he's doing the same.

It's one of those rare cold but extremely sunny

mornings in Seattle. Like a damn finger of fate pointing straight down from Heaven, a pillar of light is shining straight through the glass doors at the front of the house, landing directly on the drawer where I stowed a small, velvet-covered box not so long ago. A gift for Sloane. A gift I'm not ready to give her yet. Seems as though every time I walk past that goddamn drawer, I can feel the box inside humming like a freaking signal beacon. I really need to move it. Take it down to the gym or something. Leave it in my locker there. She'd never find it amongst all my sweat-soaked workout clothes, hand wraps and boxing gloves. But then, no. That just seems fucking wrong.

I carry the sliced pineapple upstairs on a plate, along with the eggs I've made and some fresh orange juice. Very fucking domesticated. I would never have done this for anyone else. The stars would have collided and the universe collapsed in on itself before I bowed and scraped to any other woman. I don't see taking care of my girl as bowing and scraping now, though. I see it as making sure she's fed. Making sure she's content. Making sure she's safe. Making sure she's fit and healthy enough for me to fuck her the way I like, and for her to demand more.

She's still asleep when I enter the bedroom. Her

dark hair is spilled across her pillow in loose waves around her head, her almost-black eyelashes like charcoal smudges against her pale cheeks. She looks like she's been drawn or something. Created out of thin air. I find myself thinking that a lot—that someone has crafted her, this mythical creature who's turned my life upside down—because how else can she be real? It makes no sense. The universe just isn't this kind to anyone, especially guys like me.

Placing the food down on the bedside table, I move up the bed, pulling the covers back from her body as I climb. She's naked underneath—so fucking perfect. Her breasts lay heavy, crushed between her arms as she lies on her side. I can already feel my cock stirring in my shorts. Nothing new there. Poor Sloane's eggs are going to be cold by the time she gets around to eating them. I haven't even made any food for myself. I knew *she* was all I was going to want to eat. Placing my hand on her hip, I gently turn her body so that she's on her back. Unlike my cock, her perfect nipples aren't erect yet, but I have plans on changing that. Slowly, carefully, I lower my mouth to her skin and I lick across her collarbone, moving down until I trace my tongue across the swell of her tits. So. Fucking. Amazing.

Sloane groans, body writhing a little as she surfaces into consciousness. Waking her up this way is the best goddamn part of my day. I know she's aware of what I'm doing when I feel her legs press together underneath me. She's been so good recently whenever we fuck, doing as I tell her when I tell her to without hesitation or question, that now I feel like being bad for her. She's earned it. I bite down on the now hard, tight bud of her nipple, sending a jolt of pain through her, waking her up properly. She reacts quickly, sucking in a sharp breath, her body tightening underneath me.

"Morning, angry girl. Dreaming about me?" I whisper. Her fingers wind into my hair, which is longer than it's ever been. Not hipster long. Just long enough that she can get a good fucking handful of it and pull when she wants to. She moans, which is a good sign. There aren't many women you could wake up after a twelve-hour hospital shift with a bite to the nipple and have them appreciate it. This is why we're fucking perfect together. "You planning on backing that up?" she mumbles, her voice still a little hoarse.

"What? This?" I bite her again, this time on the other nipple. Her eyelids fly open wide, her back arching off the bed. "Stay still, angry girl. Don't you dare fucking move unless I tell you to. If you're good, I'll make you come. Would you like that? Would that make you feel better?"

"Yes," she says breathlessly. "I think it would."

I hold myself over her, lowering myself a little more so that I can speak directly into her ear. "Okay. Spread your legs for me, Sloane," I growl. She shivers in that way she does. The way that lets me know she likes the sound of my voice, rough and right up close in her ear like that. She likes feeling my breath on her skin. Like the good fucking girl she is, she widens her legs for me, and I change positions, moving so I'm inside her legs now. My dick is so hard I'm pretty sure you could break rocks with it. I catch sight of her pussy and my balls begin to ache like they haven't been emptied in months, instead of yesterday morning.

Fuck.

"You're so fucking perfect," I groan. "God. Your pussy is beautiful. So pink. So sweet." I can smell her, that peculiar yet addicting scent that drives me absolutely crazy. I just want to bury my face between her legs and go to town. Not yet, though. "You want me to make you wet, angry girl?" I ask.

Sloane looks up at me with those big brown eyes of hers and nods. "I'm already wet," she whispers. She used to sound ashamed of the fact when she admitted that to me, but not anymore. She knows how much it turns me on to see her dripping wet and ready for me. As if to prove the point, she rocks her hips upward, giving me a better view.

"You're breaking the rules," I inform her. "I didn't say you could move." Palming her right breast, I squeeze hard, tightrope walking that boundary between enjoyable pain and real discomfort. I'm going easy on her, though. She's still not feeling one hundred percent, after all. Sloane's hips press back down into the mattress in an instant, her eyes closing as she breathes through what I'm doing to her. "That's better. Yeah. Good girl…" I let my other hand trail down the side of her body, my fingers slowly working toward the apex of her thighs. I don't go straight for her clit, though. I run my fingers up the insides of the legs, over her hips, up her stomach, breasts, neck, over her high cheekbones and over her lips.

"Suck," I tell her.

She obeys, opening her mouth, allowing me to slide my fingers inside. Her mouth is hot and wet, and has my cock throbbing so hard. She's so good at blowing me now. She had no clue what she was doing the very first time back in that darkened hotel room, but her inexperience and her tight mouth had almost been enough to make me come on the spot. Now that she knows what she's doing with that tongue of hers, she has the power to rob me of all fucking common sense.

She grazes her teeth against my knuckles and I can imagine all too well what that would feel like if it were my cock in her mouth. I can't help but hiss as she sucks harder. "You're being so good," I whisper into her hair. I let go of her breast and prop myself up on one elbow so I can slide my fingers from her mouth and place them between her legs, wetting her with her own saliva.

"Fuck, Zeth." Her head kicks back, rocking to one side as I work my fingertips in small, tight, purposeful circles over her clit. She's staring at me, beautiful, so turned on I can see it in her eyes, when I lift my fingers to my own mouth and slide them inside. She tastes so fucking good. Guys say that about girls all the time, but I really fucking mean it. The taste of her pussy on my tongue is enough to send the blood roaring through my veins like combustion fuel in a high-powered engine. I feel like I could do zero to a hundred in less than a second.

"Fuck, Sloane. You're incredible. Lift your knees for me. *Now.*" She bridges her legs, feet pressed flat against the bed, and holds them there. I know she wants to let her knees fall to the sides, opening herself up for me, but she's good. She waits.

That clamp from yesterday enters my head, stowed safely back in the black duffel I keep in the bottom of the wardrobe, but I reject that idea. I do want to make her moan. I do want to make her twitch. But I want my head between her legs, too, and I can't lick her with that thing in the way.

My eyes catch on the plate I brought up here with me and I know what I'm going to do. Reaching over, I pick up a piece of the pineapple and throw it into my mouth. Tastes so sweet it twinges at the sides of my tongue. "Mmm, yeah, baby. You're gonna like this, and so am I," I say. Sloane fights back a surprised smile as I take another piece of the pineapple and I head down between her legs.

I'm not in the mood to be careful. Fuck that. Shoving her knees apart myself, I get down there and take hold of her ankles, throwing her legs over my shoulders. "Are you ready, angry girl?"

She bites her lip, her head rolling back. I know she wants to arch her back off the bed again, lift her hips up to meet my mouth, but she knows there'll be consequences if she does. I'll tease the fuck out of her for hours and I won't let her come, and that's not something she enjoys. Me, on the other hand… torturing her like that gives me a particular thrill that no amount of breakfast making and domesticated life will be able to tamp down.

I bite carefully down on the piece of cold pineapple and press it into her pussy with my mouth. She gasps, hands tightening as I work it up and down, slowly tracing it from the entrance to her pussy all the way up to her clit. I want to pump my fingers inside her. I want to make her fucking scream. I can be patient when the situation calls for it, though. Instead I tease her with the piece of fruit, enjoying the flavor of it mixed in with the slick juices of her tight, amazing pussy.

I can't help myself. I have to touch myself. Reaching down, I slide my hand inside my boxers and I take hold of my cock, squeezing the tip. Feels fucking amazing, but I know sinking myself balls deep into the woman in this bed is going to be a million times better. I'm already planning where I'm going to come. Over her tits. In her mouth. Her stomach. Her back. I want to mark her all over with my come, rub it into her skin. Into her pussy. Claim her as mine.

I swallow the pineapple, and then I set to working my tongue over Sloane's clit. The fruit was fun, but I don't need it anymore. I just need her pussy in my mouth and her come on my tongue. And I'm gonna make it fucking happen right now.

Carefully, I push my index finger inside her, teasing myself as much as her with how slowly I do it. She's trembling violently by the time I'm knuckle deep. She's so tight. I'll never get over how incredible her body is. How tightly she squeezes my cock when I'm inside her.

I can't wait to get to that point. First, I let myself pump her with my fingers, knowing she's imagining they're my cock. I go slow at first but then pick up speed, matching the motion with the sweeps of my tongue over her swollen clit. I could suck on the hot bundle of nerves and make her explode, I know I could. But I refrain. This is just too much fucking fun.

She's begging me to let her come by the time I give in. And she really does fucking explode. I lick and suck at her, groaning like a goddamn savage as she comes all over my tongue. So. Fucking. Hot. She buries her hands in my hair and grinds up against me, her body shaking, falling apart as she climaxes.

I have absolutely no self-control after that. As soon as the tension falls out of her body, her muscles sinking heavy into the mattress, I grab hold of her hips and spin her over, throwing her onto her front and then lifting her hips so that her ass is in the air. "We're not done yet, angry girl." I lay my hand against her skin, making a sharp cracking sound as my palm connects with the soft curve of her ass.

"Fuck!" she gasps out, instinctively grabbing hold of the bed sheets, like she knows how hard I'm about to fuck her. Like she knows she's about to be seeing stars. I lose the boxers, and then there's nothing between me and my angry girl. I trace my cock from her clit upward, gauging her reaction, seeing where she wants me to stop…where she wants me the most. I don't even make it to her ass. She's pushing back against me, panting hard as I tease the tip of my dick against the opening of her pussy.

"You want me, Sloane? How bad do you want me inside you right now?"

"Fuck. Please. Please… please… I need you," she moans.

I could wait, I could play with her some more, but my balls feel like they're going to burst. I slam myself home, not holding back, fire singing through my veins as Sloane screams out my name.

My fingers dig into her hips as I pull her back against me. She doesn't resist. She moves with me, sighing and melting against me as I thrust so hard I'm seeing stars myself. When we come, we come together, and we're both incoherent.

Just. Too. Good.

We collapse together onto the bed as one, me still inside her, my body angled slightly to the side to keep my weight off her. When we've both regained our breath, I begin tracing my fingers absentmindedly up and down her side. Her skin is soft as silk. "You bought weird fruit," I whisper into her hair.

She laughs, and the feel of it travels through her and into me, spreading some deep, strange contentment down into my bones. This woman is going to be the end of me. "Yeah, well, I need vitamins so I can get better. But I also did it for you," she says.

"Oh? How d'you figure that?"

"They say…" She seems bemused. "They say that if you eat lots of pineapple, it makes you taste good."

The irony of what she's said hits me full on, given that I've just used a piece of it between her legs. I bite lightly on her shoulder, growling. "You don't need to eat anything to taste good, Sloane. I'm addicted to how you taste, just as you are."

She laughs. "Well, since you spend about ninety percent of your day with your head between my legs, I just wanted to make sure you enjo—" The sound of my burner ringing on the bedside table cuts her off. We both just look at it. Before earlier this morning when the Barbieri brothers called me, the thing hasn't rung in…in fucking forever. Since shit went down with my ex-employer and everything changed. And now it's ringing again? Bets are on it being Theo again. I do *not* want to talk to him. I don't want to talk to anyone who might be asking me to beat the ever-loving shit out of anyone, or worse. It's not as though I've gone soft. I'll still tear anyone limb from limb should the situation require it, but it's more on an as needed basis. For protection and defense as opposed to for money.

Sloane presses her face into the pillow, and a muffled, "You'd better get that," reaches my ears. I do answer, but only because the people who are likely to call my burner aren't the kind of people who give up after calling once.

When I hear the voice on the other end of the line, I find that the Barbieri situation has been escalated up the ranks. Typical. First Lowell's trying to ruin my fucking day, and now more of this shit. "Zeth," Roberto Barbieri, the Barber of Brooklyn himself, says. "I hear you didn't much like talking to my sons?"

"I'm more of an email kind of guy these days."

"Good to know. I'll make sure to forward you the details of our arrangement in a message once our conversation is over, then. Does that suit you?"

"And what arrangement might that be? I

already told Theo, I'm not working for anyone else anymore." I don't like this guy's tone of voice. I sure as fuck don't like how he's ruining my post-orgasm glow. Sloane's watching me with wide eyes, clearly able to hear what's being said. There's a time not too long ago when I would have left the room, but not anymore. I don't hide anything from her these days. She knows all about the fights, the underground gambling and the occasional gun deal that goes down at the fighting gym I run. She knows me, knows who I am, and knows I will never live on the straight and narrow like other, normal people. She can handle fights and dirty money so long as I'm not getting hurt. And she can handle the guns so long as I don't get my ass shot.

I doubt very much she'd handle me going out on task for the Barber of Brooklyn, though.

"Zeth, you and I both know this sedentary life you're leading isn't what you were built for. You're a cutthroat, just like I am. I'm coming for Seattle. You must have known someone would eventually. I'm laying out my cards here and now. New York is where the throne of my empire rests. I can't be in two places at once. I needbsomeone to run my west coast operations, and I want that someone to be you."

"I have no interest in being your understudy,

Roberto. Absolutely no fucking interest whatsoever." The guy is crazy if he thinks I'm putting myself into yet another position like I was in with Charlie. You don't climb out from underneath the shit heap only to voluntarily climb back under again.

"I can understand your reluctance, Zeth, I really can. But you are a very dangerous individual. If I place someone else in charge over there, I wouldn't be able to allow a man like you to be operating in the same district. It wouldn't be smart business."

"I'm not operating. I run a few fights and broker a few deals. You don't need to concern yourself with what I'm doing, Roberto. I'm none of your fucking business."

"And what about the lovely young Ms. Romera? Will she end up being my business? I fear she will if we can't find a way to make both of us happy right now."

Sloane sits up, clearly having heard her name. She looks mildly concerned, which makes my blood boil. Who does this guy think he fucking is, threatening her to get his own way? I won't allow it. I will burn down his whole fucking New York empire before I let that happen. "You don't say her name. You don't *ever* say her name," I growl.

"Don't forget who you're talking to right now,

boy. I'm bigger and I'm badder than Charlie Holsan ever was. When I offer someone a title within my organization, they fucking jump," he spits. "And this isn't just any old title. I'm offering to make you the motherfucking king of the west coast. You'd be answerable to no one but me. You need to think about this for a couple of hours, Zeth. Bear in mind, I don't make these kinds of calls personally very often. It's unlikely I'll be making another one. You should also bear in mind that I am *not* someone to be fucked with."

I laugh, and it feels raw in my throat. Caustic, poisonous laughter that gives away what I think of his threats before I can put my thoughts into words. "I vowed after Charlie that I would never be answerable to anyone ever again. And I won't. I don't want to be the king of the west coast or anywhere else for that matter. And something *you* should bear in mind, Roberto? I *am* a dangerous individual. And people don't usually live to tell the tale after fucking with *me* either."

MASON

Wanda wouldn't let me take Millie to school this morning. Said I'd terrify the poor kid if I showed up bloodied and bruised the way I am. I don't know what she thinks I'm going to do between now and the end of the day to fix the problem—as far as I know, cuts and scrapes take a little longer than an afternoon to heal— but there you go. She sent me on my way, and a part of me felt guilty about heading straight to work. I felt even guiltier when I realized I was singing in the car.

Mac nearly drops his coffee when he sees me. "Holy fucking hell, boy, what happened to your face?"

"Fought at French's," I mumble through my split lip. No point in lying to him. Mac knows everything, has his finger in so many pies. Wouldn't surprise me if he actually made some money off my ass last night somehow.

"So you'll fight in a stinking basement but you won't earn three times the money driving a car across the city for me, is that it?" he says.

"Pretty much."

"Well, whatever. I hope the other guy looks worse, I guess. Though, I don't see how *that* would be possible."

The morning goes fast. I can't wait to head over to the gym after work and train. I need to stretch out my muscles, make sure I don't completely lock up. If I want to fight again in six days, I have to make sure my whole body isn't completely jacked from not doing anything with it.

I spend the day working on Kaya's beater of a car. The old Chevy is fucked, needs scrapping entirely, but I just do what I'm told and go about fixing the damn thing. Late in the afternoon, when I jump in to turn the engine over, the interior smells just like she did yesterday—like flowers and jasmine. My dick stirs in my pants at the scent. So fucking inappropriate. I'm not supposed to be thinking about her let alone fantasizing what it would be like to be on top of her, to feel like I'm wrapping myself around her, slowly pushing myself deeper and deeper inside of her.

I have to sit in the car for an extra five minutes before my hard on eventually goes away.

Mac, the asshole, keeps me back half an hour to finish up a rushed job that comes in late. That cuts into my gym time before I need to collect Millie, but whatever. Something is better than nothing. I'm jogging across the street, gym bag in hand, when a sleek black Audi rolls up out the front of the gym. The window buzzes down and a stern looking woman with bright blonde hair and cold blue eyes is staring straight at me. For a moment I think she's about to ask for directions out of this sketchy part of town—people get lost here all the time—but then she does something that makes my stomach drop through the floor. She pulls out a badge.

"Agent Lowell," she says. "DEA. You're Mason Reeves, right? Got time to have a little chat?"

A million things immediately flash through my

head, paralysing me. I manage to keep my face a mask of calm, however. "Not really. I kind of have somewhere I need to be."

"That's a pity. See my colleague here was just telling me that we should come over to your place, investigate a tip off we had."

"What kind of tip off?"

"Apparently, you're involved in a little drug running for your boss there." Agent Lowell gestures to Mac, who is just pulling down the roller shutter on the building behind me. Mac sees Lowell and his eyes go wide. Slowly, carefully, he lifts his right hand and flips her off. "Awww. Mac remembers me," Agent Lowell says, smiling.

"I don't run drugs for him. I work on the cars, and then I go home. End of story."

"Oh?" The woman frowns up at me, tilting her head to one side. "And what's with the face, then? You get those bruises from *fixing cars*?"

"No. I was in a fight.

"French's, right?" Lowell grins. "Yeah, I've heard a lot about the place. That's Seattle PD's domain normally, but could be there are drugs there, too, right, Agent Cooper?"

The guy next to her sitting at the wheel grunts, squinting at me from inside the car. "Could be."

"And even if there aren't any drugs, participating in an underground fighting ring's pretty dangerous, wouldn't you say? Not to mention illegal. Would CPS consider a young guy involved in blood sports a fit role model for a little girl?"

My blood runs ice-cold in my veins. "Don't fucking threaten me."

"Oh, come on, now. I'm not threatening you. I just want to ask you a few questions. Won't take a moment of your time."

"What about? I've told you, I haven't done anything wrong."

"It's not you we're interested in, Mr. Reeves. I can promise you that. We're actually more interested in what you know about Zeth Mayfair."

Zeth? Well, now that makes a little more sense. I'm not completely stupid, though. I talk to this woman about Zeth Mayfair and I'm going to end up in a ditch somewhere, missing body parts. "Look, I'm really sorry. I don't know what you heard but I don't know anything about Mayfair. I go to his gym sometimes. That's it."

Lowell shakes her head, her lips pulling into a taut line. "Don't be foolish, Mason. Everyone in Seattle knows *something* about Zeth. You want to know what *I* know?"

"Not particularly." I look away, toward the gym, hoping against hope that the man himself hasn't seen me out here talking to a federal agent. I'm shit out of luck, though. He's leaning against the wall inside the gym, arms folded across his chest, eyes fixed solely on me as I shift from foot to foot.

"Don't worry about him," Lowell says. "Zeth's headed back to Chino any day now. He just doesn't know it yet. See, we found a body last week up in the mountains. The body of a young woman. Gun shot wound." Lowell glances over at Zeth, still leaning against the wall. She shoots him an unbearably sweet smile, and then waves.

"The girl was murdered, Mr. Reeves," she says, still smiling. "And guess who's DNA was *all* over her."

ALSO BY CALLIE HART

FREE TO READ ON KINDLE UNLIMITED!

DARK, SEXY, AND TWISTED! A BAD BOY WHO WILL CLAIM BOTH YOUR HEART AND YOUR SOUL.

Read the entire Blood & Roses Series

FREE on Kindle Unlimited!

WANT TO DISAPPEAR INTO THE DARK, SEDUCTIVE WORLD OF AN EX-PRIEST TURNED HITMAN?

Read the Dirty Nasty Freaks Series

FREE on Kindle Unlimited!

LOVE A DARK AND DANGEROUS MC STORY? NEED TO KNOW WHAT HAPPENED TO SLOANE'S SISTER?

Read the Dead Man's Ink Boxset

FREE on Kindle Unlimited!

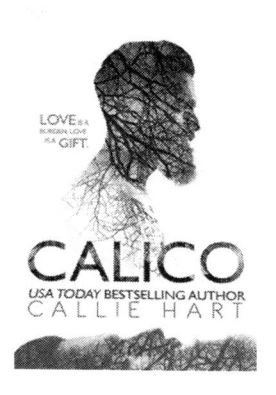

WANT AN EMOTIONAL, DARK, TWISTED STANDALONE?

Read Calico!

FREE on Kindle Unlimited

WANT A PLOT THAT WILL TAKE YOUR BREATH AWAY?

Read Between Here and the Horizon

FREE on Kindle Unlimited!

WANT A NYC TALE OF HEARTBREAK, NEW LOVE, AND A HEALTHY DASH OF VIOLENCE?

Read Rooke

FREE on Kindle Unlimited!

KEEP READING TO CHECK OUT THE PROLOGUE TO THE REBEL OF RALEIGH HIGH!

Grave robbery has never been that high on my to-do list, but tonight, with a frigid Washington wind blowing in off Lake Cushman, I find myself up to my waist in dirt with a shovel in my hand. Weird how life likes to fuck with you sometimes. There are plenty of other places I could be tonight, and yet here I am, the muscles in my back aching like a bitch as I lift the haft of the shovel over my head and I pile-drive the steel blade into the unforgiving, frozen earth.

"Dorme, Passerotto. Shhh. Time to go to sleep."

I ignore the soft whisper in my ear. That voice is long gone now. It doesn't serve me to remember it, but...forgetting wouldn't be right. Forgetting would feel like a betrayal.

The cut, scrape, swish of my work fills the night air, and a river of sweat courses down my spine. My body's no stranger to physical labor, and I'm grateful for the fact as I press forward, hurling clods of icy dirt over my bare shoulder and out of the deepening hole. This task would be way shittier if I weren't in shape. Scratch that...it'd probably be impossible.

I don't believe in zombies, vampires, ghosts, or any other kind of apparition, but there's something about this place that creeps me out. *Yeah, it's a graveyard, Poindexter. You're surrounded by rotting bodies.* I roll my eyes at my own inner monologue, again lobbing loose grave soil out onto the well-manicured grass to my right. It's only natural that this place would have a sinister edge to it. It's abandoned, not a soul in sight (very convenient for me), and yet there are signs of the living everywhere—laminated cards bearing the smiling faces of children; floral tributes, tinged with the first signs of fading decay; stuffed animals, fur matted and crusted over with frost. The people who left these trinkets and treasures are safe in their own warm houses now, though. It feels like the end of the world out here, a neglected place, filled with neglected memories. The moon overhead, round and fat in the clear September sky, casts long shadows, making spears out of the headstones.

I wipe at my forehead with the back of my forearm, grit and clay smearing my skin, and I consider how much further down I need to go. They bury people deeper than usual here in Grays Harbor County. I read that on the cemetery website yesterday morning when I was scoping the place. They said it was because of the bears. Seriously fucked up. I try not to think about that as I quicken my pace, eager to accomplish my goal and get the hell out of here.

A loud, metallic clang eventually signals that I've come to the end of the road, I've found what I'm looking for, and that hard part, the disturbing-as-fuck part of this evening's adventure has finally arrived. Takes some time to clear off the coffin and figure out how to open the damn thing. This kind of thing is always made to look so easy in the movies, but it's not. Far from it. I nearly rip the damn nail from my index finger as I try to heave back the lid.

"*Figlio di puttana!* Fucking piece of shit." I nearly shove my finger into my mouth to suck on it, but then I remember the fucking grave dirt underneath the nail of the finger in question and I decide against it. Dirt is dirt is dirt, but grave dirt? No, thanks.

Upon close inspection, I conclude there's no way to finesse the coffin open, so I resort to brute force, heaving on the wood until the coffin makes a splintering sound and the lid frees, groaning as it yawns reluctantly open.

Inside: the body of a man in his late fifties, dressed in a red button-down shirt and a black tie. No suit jacket. His face, a face I know all too well, is as severe and downturned in death as it was in life. Hooked nose; pronounced brow; deep, cavernous lines carved into the flesh of his cheeks, bracketing his thin-lipped, angry-looking mouth. His hands have been stacked on top of his chest. Beneath them: a copy of the Gideon's Bible. The cheap, generic kind you might find in the drawer of a nightstand in a Motel 6. I scowl at the sight, a familiar, slick, oily knot tightening in my chest. Ahh, rage, my friend. Fancy seeing you here, you sly old fuck.

Speaking to a dead body isn't nearly as weird as you might think. "Well, Gary. Looks like the piper wanted to be paid, huh?" Sweat stings at my eyes. Crouching down, feet balanced on either side of the coffin, I take my t-shirt from my back pocket where I hung it for safe keeping, and I use it to wipe at my face. Before I arrived here tonight, I'd prepared myself for the sickly-sweet odor of death, was ready to face it, but two feet away from Gary, the only thing I can smell are the winter pine trees on the wind. "Figured we'd end up here eventually," I tell him. "Didn't think it would be so soon, but hey… I'm not complaining."

Unsurprisingly, Gary has very little say in return.

I contemplate his face. His sallow, sunken in cheeks and his pinched, withered features. When did he get so gaunt? Was he always like that, or did the process of dying shave twenty pounds off the guy? I suppose it's a mystery I'll never solve now. It's been six months since I saw him last; there's every chance the bastard joined Jenny Craig during that time.

I stoop low over him and reach out a finger, prodding at his cheek, expecting to find some give in him, but there's nothing. He's solid. Stiff, like a calcified husk. Like I said, I didn't come here unprepared. Gary's been dead for four days, so it seemed prudent to read up on what kind of shape the motherfucker was going to be in when I unearthed him. His corpse isn't bloated, though. His tongue isn't protruding from between his teeth. He looks… he looks kind of normal. Even the makeup they must have put on him at the funeral home still looks like it's holding up.

It's the cold. Has to be. There's no way he'd be so perfectly preserved otherwise. Honestly, I'm a little disappointed. A part of me was looking forward to seeing the bastard's skin sloughing from his bones.

With quick hands I get to work, first grabbing the Bible and tossing it out of the grave, hissing between my teeth. Gary's hands are next. I wrench them apart, then hinge his arms down by his sides, giving me room to unbutton his shirt and fold the material back. He's wearing a vest, but that's no big deal. I stand briefly so I can get my hand in my pocket, and then the short blade of my flick knife is gleaming brilliantly in the moonlight. The sharpened steel cuts through the thin polyester in two seconds flat.

Gary's narrow, twisted pigeon chest hasn't been

rouged up like his face, and here I find the evidence of decay I was looking for. His skin's pale, tinged an unhealthy blue, mottled like a fine-veined marble. And just off center of his torso, a little up and to the right, a small, neat, black hole with puckered edges punctures his skin.

Do morticians charge for sewing gunshot wounds closed? If they do, then Gary's penny-pinching brother from Mississauga declined to cover the added expense. I never met him—the brother. In the three years I lived under the roof of Gary Quincy's doublewide trailer, I only ever heard his brother's voice on the other end of a telephone, and even then I knew I didn't like the fucker.

"Had to make sure, Gaz," I say. "Needed to see with my own two eyes. Now. Where'd you put it, hmm?" I pat down the pockets of his cheap suit pants, feeling around carefully…

I didn't just come here to make sure Gary Quincy was dead, though that was a big part of this. I've spent the last two hours laboring in the dirt, digging his ass up, because he has something that belongs to me, something he took from me, and I want it back.

His pockets are empty. Juuuust fucking perfect. I lift his head, checking his throat, just to make sure, but it's not there, either.

"You swallow it, Gary?" I ask, glancing at the knife I rested on the edge of the coffin. "Wouldn't put it past you, you fucking psycho." I take up the knife, dread lacing my bones as I survey the concave shell of his stomach, wondering if I have the stones to even proceed with such a fucking crazy idea. Cutting Gary open, unraveling his intestines, feeling around inside the cavities, nooks and crannies of his insides will not be something I'll ever be able to forget. Something like that changes a person, I'm betting, and I don't really feel like undertaking that type of a transformation right now. I like being able to sleep at night.

"Dorme, Passerotto. Shhh. Time to go to sleep."

Fuck. No, not here. Not now. I push the voice aside, shivering away from the comforting warmth of it, and I'm left chilled to my core, a cold, angry fist closing around my heart.

"Fuck you, Gary," I growl under my breath. "It wasn't yours. You should have known I wouldn't let you keep it." Steeling myself, I pick up the knife and lower the blade, its shining tip hovering an inch above Gary's stomach. I'm ready. I can do this. I'll gut him from stem to sternum if it means I can reclaim what's mine.

The knife meets Gary's skin, and…

The moonlight strengthens for a second, the

shadows inside the grave peeling back, and I catch an unexpected flash of gold out of the corner of my eye. A brisk gust of wind moans through the trees, and I stop dead.

There...in Gary's right hand.

"Motherfucker," I hiss. "I knew it. Couldn't just leave it for me, could you? Had to make sure I never found it." Prizing Gary's fingers open takes work. I don't even flinch when I feel the snap of his middle finger breaking, though. I actually have to fight the macabre urge to break even more of his bones as I pluck the small gold medallion attached to the delicate gold chain out of his palm and close my own hand around it.

Suddenly, I'm five years old again, watching owl-eyed as a woman with hair the color of sunshine kisses the small, golden medallion and tucks it inside her shirt. "St. Christopher, holy patron of travelers, protect and lead me safely on my journey."

Jesus, the past is hitting hard tonight. It's as if my close proximity to Gary's empty carcass is opening all kinds of doors to the dead, and I can't fucking take it a moment longer. Standing, freezing cold now that I've been still for a while and my sweat has cooled, I adopt a wide stance with my feet still planted on either side of the coffin, and I unzip my fly. "Sorry, Gary. But you and I both know you deserve this."

Steam rises from the coffin as my piss splashes down onto Gary's chest. I've been waiting for this for a long, long time. It feels…Damn, it feels fucking—

"Hold it right there, kid. Stop what you're doing this instant!"

Oh, come on.

I tense, freezing in place, every part of me rigid.

The female voice behind me is alive with anger as she repeats her command. "I said stop what you're doing, asshole!"

I risk a glance over my shoulder and my stomach sinks when I see the uniform. The badge. The gun aimed at the back of my head. "If you're referring to the fact that I'm still pissing, Officer, then I'm afraid there's nothing I can do. Stopping mid-flow is bad for the prostate." I smile to myself, knowing I'm not helping matters. Fuck it though, right? I am going to be arrested. No doubt about it. And if my ass is getting thrown in jail for this, then I'll be damned if I don't finish what I started.

"Kid, if you don't quit right now and put your dick away, you're gonna get Tazed. You understand me?"

Ahh. Tazer, not a gun. Well, I guess that's something. I surrender a long, resigned sigh. I do not stop.

"Last chance, dumbass."

There are worst things to be in this life than stubborn and dedicated to a cause. And let's face it…this opportunity will never present itself again. I brace, even though bracing is pointless, and I wait for the pain.

When it comes, lancing into my back, striking like lightning down my arms and into my legs, I retain just enough control to make sure I sag sideways into Gary's grave and not forwards.

After all, the very last thing I need, on the back of such a long and successful night, is to find myself slumped over the deceased remains of the man who repeatedly beat me while lying in a pool of my own piss.

Somehow, through my gritted teeth, my tensed muscles, and the blinding ball of pain that's lashed itself to my back, I manage to choke out a single, bitter burst of laughter.

The sound echoes like a gunshot over midnight Lake Cushman.

ABOUT THE AUTHOR

USA Today Bestselling Author, Callie Hart, was born in England, but has lived all over the world. As such, she has a weird accent that generally confuses people. She currently resides in Los Angeles, California, where she can usually be found hiking, practicing yoga, kicking ass at Cards Against Humanity, or watching re-runs of Game of Thrones.

To sign up for her newsletter, click here.

FOLLOW ME ON INSTAGRAM!

The best way to keep up to date with all of my upcoming releases and some other VERY exciting secret projects I'm currently working on is to follow me on Instagram! Instagram is fast becoming my favorite way to communicate with the outside world, and I'd love to hear from you over there. I do answer my direct messages (though it might take me some time) plus I frequently post pics of my mini Dachshund, Cooper, so it's basically a win/win.

You can find me right here!

Alternatively, you can find me via me handle @calliehartauthor within the app.

I look forward to hanging out with you!

Callie
x

Printed in Great Britain
by Amazon